It was not an

Kyle was about t...
ing her. Briony'...
should stop the e...
at the back of her skirt. But she didn't want to
stop him, Briony acknowledged to herself,
while the rational part of her mind was
appalled by the desperate need in her that
could make her want Kyle's touch, no matter
how impersonal, on her body.

Dear Reader

Welcome to Barra! Yes, this month we pay a visit to colder but no less enchanting climes. Scotland must be one of the most romantic countries on earth, with its stirring pageant of history, the incomparable beauty of its scenery, and its famous hospitality. . .all these qualities — and more — are encapsulated in the remote corner that is Barra. Why not discover it for yourself. . .?

The Editor

The author says:

'Of all the enchanting islands of the Hebrides, Barra is my first love. Beauty, history, traditions — and the sheer romance of a daily life lived against the backdrop of a castle in the sea: this tiny island has it all, and I've chosen it as the setting for my story to share its romance, and the spell it has cast on me.'

Edwina Shore

★ TURN TO THE BACK PAGES OF THIS BOOK FOR *WELCOME TO EUROPE*. . .OUR FASCINATING FACT-FILE ★

DARK SIDE OF
THE ISLAND

BY

EDWINA SHORE

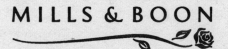

MILLS & BOON

MILLS & BOON LIMITED
ETON HOUSE, 18–24 PARADISE ROAD
RICHMOND, SURREY, TW9 1SR

To Mairi, Ishabel, and to Barra, with love.

First published in Great Britain 1994
by Mills & Boon Limited

© Edwina Shore 1994

Australian copyright 1994
Philippine copyright 1994
This edition 1994

ISBN 0 263 78508 4

Set in 10½ on 12 pt Linotron Times
01-9406-49966

Typeset in Great Britain by Centracet, Cambridge
Made and printed in Great Britain

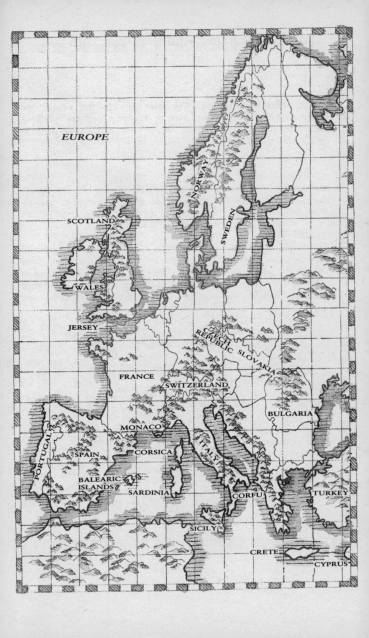

EUROPE

SCOTLAND

WALES

JERSEY

NORWAY

SWEDEN

CZECH
REPUBLIC SLOVAKIA

FRANCE

SWITZERLAND

BULGARIA

MONACO

PORTUGAL

SPAIN

CORSICA

ITALY

BALEARIC
ISLANDS

SARDINIA

CORFU

TURKEY

SICILY

CRETE

CYPRUS

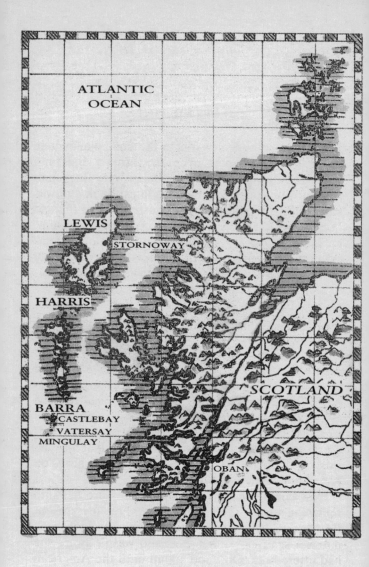

CHAPTER ONE

BRIONY thought she saw him as the small plane made its first, slow swoop over the airport building. Kyle. . .? But it couldn't have been. Kyle Buchanan was in New York promoting his latest book and was scheduled to fly straight on to Australia after that, so Derek had assured her, and she had believed him; her business partner's sources of information were as extensive as they were mysterious, and invariably infallible. Briony unfroze a little from her shock.

The second circuit was lower, slower, and this time as the plane buzzed past the upturned faces on the ground she saw him clearly and distinctly, a tall, dark figure standing behind the main huddle of the waiting crowd. The man she had thought looked like Kyle *was* Kyle, and her heart nearly stopped in the moment of shocked realisation that her husband was not in New York as Derek had thought, but here on Barra, and in another few moments the plane would be down and crunching over the cockleshells towards the building. And towards Kyle and a meeting she was nowhere near ready for, least of all here, on Kyle's home territory.

How could she have let Derek pressure her into returning to the Outer Hebrides? For any reason. Briony couldn't believe it of herself. She sank back into her seat, closed her eyes and wasn't aware she had uttered the 'Oh, God' aloud until the American voice on the other side of the tiny aisle made her start.

'I know how you feel. I've never landed on a beach before either,' the blonde, middle-aged woman laughed nervously.

Briony flashed her a mechanical smile. The woman couldn't begin to imagine how she felt. Briony wasn't sure herself now that the first impact of the shock had passed, unnerved, unprepared. . .angry — with Derek, yes, but more with herself for having gone along with his plans.

'It simply has to be Barra, Briony, because I've chosen it for the showing of our Hebridean Collection and all but finalised the arrangements with the buyers. You know this is our big chance to break into the US, so surely you must see how absolutely essential it is that you put the feel of the place into your wonderful designs right from the start.' Derek Saunders could bully and flatter in the same breath, and he spoke of their 'Hebridean Collection' as if it were already in existence, and not just a series of exciting images searing in and out of her mind, still yet to transform themselves into preliminary sketches.

Derek's mind was nine months ahead of hers, and utterly consumed by his determination to capture the elusive American market, and Briony had to admit that his novel idea to use the island's quaint main street as a real live catwalk for the showing next April had all the hallmarks of a winner. Beyond the end of the tiny street, and straight out of a fairy-tale, sat a small, solid castle in the sea; with that sort of captivating background for a collection, Derek could probably have enticed buyers into ordering a new line in charity shop rejects.

She wanted the collection to be a success just as much as Derek, and possibly more, so in the end, and reassured by his insistence that Kyle would be away, Briony had put her reservations aside and agreed that Barra was the ideal place to start work on the sketches. She loved the remote Scottish island, and, in spite of everything, was looking forward to the prospect of creating a special winter range solely in cashmere and tweed, lifting the wonderful fabrics out of their usually sedate place in the fashion world and turning them into something vital and exciting. 'Breathing life into them', was how Derek put it. After checking out the cashmeres in Hawick on the Scottish mainland, she had spent a week on the islands of Harris and Lewis looking at tweeds and was ready to begin on the designs, but with Kyle on the island her proposed two-week stay was out of the question now, and her only thought to head back to the mainland and London, on the very next plane. *If* she managed to get a seat on to Glasgow today, and she didn't think much of her chances if this full flight from Lewis to Barra was any indication.

'Say, that was kinda fun.'

Briony glanced at the woman and then swung her eyes to the window. They were down and she had not noticed, missing out on the thrill of the exotic landing on the Traigh Mhor, Gaelic for 'big beach,' and the only place on the island flat enough for a small twenty-seater plane to land at low tide. The tourists considered it a major plus. She could see cameras everywhere; she could also see Kyle, really close now, and, in spite of herself, her nerves, the tension, Briony was conscious of the familiar quickening of her heartbeat.

It always happened. . .the quickened beat, the catch of breath, in those first moments of seeing him. Even when she saw him on television that instant of physical attraction was all at once there, as if she was caught off guard by Kyle's dark, brooding good looks. It had been like that from their first meeting a little over three and a half years ago, and it was ironic that she should still react the same way when their marriage was all but over, if only she could bring herself to face it.

He was wearing his frowning, impatient expression as he scanned over the tops of the heads in front of him, his thick black waves lifting and fluttering this way and that in the wind. Briony watched him brush an impatient hand across his forehead to push the hair out of his eyes, then as he was dropping the hand he raised it again abruptly in a quick wave, his expression changing with the sudden smile that lit up his face and softened the almost intimidating hardness of his features.

He used to smile like that on his first glimpse of her coming around the side of the plane, or if he'd caught sight of her at her window seat, as he sometimes did. Who was it now that he seemed so pleased to see? Briony couldn't tell and turned away from the window just as the tiny old man from the seat in front of her was scooping up her large soft leather handbag-cum-carryall from beside her feet.

'It'll be easier for you to get out if I carry this for

you, lass,' he smiled with not very many teeth, but with a warmth that, with his voice, identified him immediately as a local.

Too late to tell him she didn't want to get out at all and had intended to stay in the plane as long as she possibly could to avoid Kyle. Now she had to follow her bag, keeping her head bent so as not to bang it against the low ceiling; the elderly man leading the way had no such problem.

'Thank you.' Briony reclaimed the bag at the bottom of the steps, her smile disappearing as her feet touched 'ground,' and the high-heeled strappy shoes embedded themselves in wet, gritty cockle-shells. Derek's fault — again. He had flown to Stornoway on Lewis this morning to take her to lunch and talk materials and designs before she left for Barra. Typically unpunctual, he had rushed her to the airport at the very last minute so she hadn't time to change into the sensible flat shoes in her carryall and had forgotten all about them until now, when she had to squelch her uncomfortable, not to mention inelegant way to the firmer surface of the dry shell grit around the front of the small, single-storey building.

There were a lot of people milling about but no sign of Kyle, Briony noted with relief as she dropped her bag to the ground at the corner of the building and slipped off one shoe to dislodge an extra-large bit of shell that couldn't even wait the short distance to the Ladies' in the airport lounge. She was about to wriggle her foot back into it when someone brushed against her from behind, throwing her off balance. She teetered, reaching for the wall with one hand while the other made a sort of wild little flail through the air and landed in the strong, supportive grip of whoever was coming up alongside her — the friendly bag-carrying old man, Briony thought until she jerked her head around.

'Really, Briony, you'll do yourself a mischief hopping about on one foot like that,' Kyle chided, the mocking dryness as familiar as the quirk of the corner of his mouth as he took in her shock, and seemed to enjoy it, while she just stood there staring at him, as taken unawares as if she had not had those prelanding minutes to prepare herself for the likelihood of a meeting.

'Kyle. . .' Briony found her voice in a funny half-question, half-statement that sounded as if she was testing out his name for the first time. 'Hello,' she added ridiculously brightly, and couldn't think of another thing to say. Her right hand was in his left hand so it looked as if they were holding hands — they were in fact holding hands in their first physical contact in four months, and her nerves were not up to it. Every one of them seemed to have gone haywire, and her heart was crazily out of beat again. She gave a small agitated tug.

Kyle released her hand, readily, but with a hint of a sardonic smile that told her he was fully aware of her agitation, and probably its cause. 'I beg your pardon, Henrik.' He addressed the silver-haired, distinguished-looking man hovering in front of them. 'I seem to have mislaid my manners. May I introduce Briony. . . Hayward?' The pause between names was barely noticeable but Briony didn't miss it, nor the faintly ironic emphasis on the surname, her maiden name, which she had continued to use after she had married Kyle, but only professionally, and never before had Kyle introduced her by it. Or omitted to add that she was his wife. 'Briony, this is Professor Henrik Bergen, who has come to Barra to further his research in Gaelic language and folklore.'

An elderly Norwegian academic; so this was who Kyle had been so pleased to see. Briony rallied with a smile, then felt it falter mid-handshake, and whatever was left of it stayed frozen while her eyes swerved from the professor to the girl who had come up beside Kyle and was putting her hand lightly on his arm to draw his attention to herself.

Kyle turned to her with a smile. 'Ah, here you are, Ishabel. I wondered where you'd got to. Briony, I don't believe you've met Ishabel Macleod, have you? Ishabel, Briony Hayward.'

Again Briony registered that Kyle had not introduced her as his wife. After that everything else seemed to register at once. . .that the girl was in her early twenties, and very beautiful; that she was familiar enough with Kyle to put a hand on his arm and that Kyle didn't mind; that he hadn't elaborated on who Ishabel was, nor introduced her to the professor, which had to mean he had introduced her earlier. When they'd met him off the plane together. . .?

'Hello.' The voice was soft and of the islands, if any confirmation was needed that the girl was a local.

A local Briony had never seen before, and one of those pale-skinned, dark-eyed, black-haired Celtic islanders whose visual impact could take your breath away. Like Kyle. Standing there side by side, the impact of their looks was doubled. They made an extraordinarily stunning couple, and for one alarming moment it felt as if her heart had turned over inside her chest.

'Hello, Ishabel.' Briony made an attempt to reactivate her smile. Ishabel hadn't smiled, just nodded, and, with the gesture, had let her hand slide off Kyle's arm.

'But you must attend to your shoe, my dear Miss Hayward. It must be most uncomfortable for you,' the professor was urging with a concerned glance at her feet, thereby drawing Kyle and Ishabel's eyes down to the one foot still half-in, half-out of the shoe.

Briony embarrassedly rammed her foot fully back into the shoe and as she looked up caught Ishabel's amused gaze. Like most females on Barra, the girl was in flat shoes, Briony had noticed, as she had everything else about her.

'A delight to land upon the water's edge, of course, but a nuisance for lady visitors, is it not? Your first visit to Barra, Miss Hayward?'

'No, Henrik, Ms Hayward has visited us often in the past,' Kyle took it upon himself to answer for her. 'But not for quite some time, which must account for her lapse of memory about our primitive facilities. As you see, Briony, our standard of sophistication has not improved in the. . .almost twelve months — isn't it now? — since your last visit,' he went on with smooth, mocking regret, the barb going completely over the academic's head; not so Briony's. Nor Ishabel's, as Briony could tell from those expressive dark eyes. 'Ms Hayward is a fashion designer in London,' Kyle put in like a host determined that his guests should know everything about each other.

Unlike Ishabel's frank stare, his eyes were looking her over in that disconcerting way of his, through his lashes, seeming not to look at all while he didn't miss a thing, and making her feel self-conscious and overdressed in the short, slim white linen skirt and long matching jacket over a turquoise silk camisole, Her honey-blonde hair was off her face and braided into a thick plait — a sensible precaution against the Barra breezes, yet overall Briony was aware that the image she prsented was of big-city sophistication, jarringly out of place on a remote island, and jarringly in contrast to Ishabel's casual cotton knit skirt and top, the dark blue of it several shades lighter than Kyle's navy fisherman's jersey and dark trousers.

'You're still as involved as ever in that exciting industry?'

'Yes,' Briony replied shortly to Kyle's loaded question, which might have passed for general conversation and was anything but.

'How interesting.' Henrik Bergen took his cue from Kyle and kept the conversational ball rolling. 'And have you come to Barra for the Feis too, Miss Hayward?'

'Feis?' Briony repeated as if she'd never heard of the annual two-week festival — a celebration of the island's Gaelic culture — when she knew it as well as any islander; knew to pronouce it 'Faish,' and had more than once enjoyed its concerts and dances with Kyle. She also knew it was held during the first two weeks of July, but had forgotten. The full plane and the extra-large crowd of visitors around the airport were instantly explained. 'No, I haven't come for the Feis,' she murmured, as her faint hope of getting a seat on any plane—to anywhere—for days flickered out. It would have to be the ferry now, and as for accommodation. . . With the island's limited supply, even an enforced three- or four-day stay was going to be a problem with the Feis in progress.

'Well, I'm sure you will enjoy it regardless. Where——?' Professor Bergen broke off abruptly.

Ishabel had swung away to say something in Gaelic to a woman walking past. In a moment she returned her attention, but only to Kyle. 'I have to go now.' She smiled up at him.

It was a beautiful smile as Briony would have expected, but what she had not expected was the. . . not secretiveness of it—'privateness' was the word that described it. It was as if she and the professor did not exist for Ishabel at that moment, and at that same moment Briony felt her heart give another awful lurch. Ishabel Macleod in love with Kyle. . .? Was that what she had sensed before and was sensing now? She couldn't bring herself to look at Kyle's reaction to the ravishing smile.

'Goodbye.' Ishabel divided the word unsmilingly between them—Briony and Henrik Bergen. For Kyle, it was another light touch on the arm, and she was gone, swiftly, gracefully, to catch up with the woman rounding the corner of the building and presumably on her way to the small car park behind it.

Kyle had simply said, 'Goodbye, Ishabel,'

The professor had added, 'Goodbye, Miss Macleod.' Still numbed by the girl's open display of affection towards Kyle, Briony said nothing.

'You were saying, Henrik. . .?' Kyle prompted.

'Ah, yes, I was about to enquire as to which hotel Miss Hayward is booked into. Perhaps we are to be fellow guests?'

'Ms Hayward usually stays with me,' Kyle interposed casually before Briony had a chance to answer.

Henrik Bergen looked nonplussed. 'Oh. Oh, I see.'

It was obvious he didn't see at all, and neither did Briony. Kyle's statement had her staring at him in bewilderment. Was he suggesting that after four months of not a word between them she join him at Reef House as she had always done? As if nothing had happened? As if he had not walked out on her and their marriage and left her shattered?

'Not this time, thank you, Kyle,' she refused in shaky politeness and through a forced smile that was solely for the professor's benefit.

'Oh, but I insist.' Kyle focused his own softly threatening smile on her and suddenly the charge of tension between them was too obvious for even the professor to miss.

'Will you excuse me while I go into the lounge to examine that shell mural I see through the window there? It looks most facinating.'

'How could you embarrass your friend like that?' Using the professor's embarrassment as a springboard, Briony got in first, shaken and angry that Kyle was forcing a confrontation on her—springing it on her when she was least prepared and at her most vulnerable. 'This is hardly the time or place to carry on this sort of personal discussion.' She would have snatched up her bag from the ground and escaped if Kyle hadn't anticipated her next move and stepped in closer to block any downward reach.

'I agree,' he snapped in icy staccato. 'And, while your reasons for this visit to Barra are your own business, now that you are here, and while you are here, your place is with me at Reef House.' Kyle's voice was clipped and cold; he had been educated in England, and, except when speaking Gaelic, carried no trace of the island's lilt in his natural speaking voice. However, it was only when he was really angry that the intimidating iciness took over.

Briony was too angry herself to be intimidated. With a defiant lift of the chin, she locked eyes with him, her own green exchanging fire with the blue-black. 'My. . .*place*, Kyle?' The acid she was trying for got lost in the unexpected tremor.

'Precisely. Your place. And your place while you are my wife is in my house. I mean it, Briony. I will not permit you to stay anywhere else on this island.' Kyle laid down the law without any change in the controlled coldness, which gave it more impact than any unleashed anger could have done.

'Permit?' Briony repeated the word, taken aback by the arrogance of Kyle's attitude, yet knowing that, on this island at least, she was defeated by it. She tried to hold on to her defiance, token as it was, for just a little longer. 'Appearances. That's what this is all about, isn't it? I should have realised it — that if I stay anywhere but Reef House it would be a reflection on Kyle Buchanan's reputation as lord and

master of all he owns—and that includes his wife.'
She smiled tauntingly into the hard, impassive face,
an icy mask, except for the angry glow in his eyes.

'If you want to put it that way,' Kyle said tightly.

What other way was there to put it? Kyle didn't
want her at Reef House. Didn't want her on the
island, or in his life, but she had turned up, and as
his wife she had her 'place'. *While* she was his wife.
There was a time-limit contained in the word which
Briony had not missed. She gave a small, jerky shrug,
a capitulation, and Kyle recognised it as such.

His voice changed with his victory, and in the
circumstances it was preposterous that he could
sound so normal. 'We'd better go and collect your
case from the lounge and——' He stopped, and they
both turned their heads towards the plane as its
engines revved noisily for the run across the cockle-
shells and take-off for Glasgow.

'I prefer to find my own way, thank you, and will
take a cab,' Briony told him when the noise had
retreated down the beach. 'I need to go into
Castlebay first anyway. You needn't worry.' She
laughed scratchily as Kyle's face instantly showed
suspicion. 'I can hardly escape you, can I, when the
only way I could get off this island is by swimming?
And you know I don't swim.' Without waiting for a
reply, or permission, Briony snatched up her bag at
last and hurriedly made for the entrance into the
lounge where Henrik Bergen was still tactfully hovering. 'I believe Kyle is ready to leave now. A
pleasure to have met you, Professor.' She gave him
a brief smile as she went past to the Ladies' but

guessed from his quick glance of concern that she had not managed to camouflage how shaken she was.

Nor from Kyle either if the strained white face staring back at her from the Ladies' mirror was how she had looked under the scrutiny of the intent dark eyes that had been noting her every reaction. . . every moment of her series of shocks. Noting her anger too, which was the last thing she ever wanted to be goaded into, afraid that if her anger showed, then her hurt would show through it, and *that* she had promised herself never to betray to Kyle.

Briony changed out of the strappy shoes into the flat ones because the shell grit was already chafing her stockingless feet, and because Castlebay's sloping tiny street was not designed for high heels, any more than the rest of this little island that she had to get herself off as quickly as possible.

Not until next Sunday's flight, she was told at the counter. Briony declined the seat in favour of the ferry, the more practical alternative given that her car was due from Stornoway via Oban on the mainland on Wednesday evening's ferry. She and the car could then leave on Thursday morning which meant only three nights on Barra. Three nights under Kyle's roof.

The post bus that brought mail and passengers to the plane, and carried mail and passengers from the plane, had long gone, as had the few cabs that usually met the plane, but the woman behind the counter obligingly telephoned for one, and, leaving her suitcase in the lounge, Briony went outside again to wait for it. She needed air. A tight knot seemed to have settled inside her chest in the wake of the confrontation with Kyle, a confrontation she had dreaded. Even as she had allowed herself to be persuaded into Derek's plan, she had known it was madness to risk a return to Barra. True, there was always the risk of unexpectedly running into Kyle in London, but in London 'appearances' would not have come into it, and Kyle would not have been demanding that she stay with him as he was doing now — arrogantly asserting his claim over her to the last.

As he had from the start, only then Briony had not seen it as arrogance but as evidence of his overwhelming passion. A mutual passion because she had felt exactly the same way about him, and that part of herself had come as a shock to her when she had always considered herself to be completely in control of her emotions where men were concerned.

Incredibly, the man before Kyle had been Derek. Thirty then, and the same age as Kyle, Derek owned a highly successful fabric importing business, and they had met in the course of her first job as a designer for an established fashion house. Later Derek told her that he had earmarked her right then for the fashion house he wanted to set up as a sideline to his fabric business, a good business move to combine the two, Derek had decided.

Briony suspected that he'd also decided that marrying his designer would be a good business move too. That was probably cynical of her because she knew Derek had been genuinely fond of her in his way. Blond like herself, and good-looking if too conventionally even-featured, he had been great company and a lot of fun in the beginning, but it was his boundless vitality and ambition that had really attracted her — not into falling in love with him, though, and she had easily resisted all his efforts to entice her into bed, and later into marriage. However, they had set up their small fashion house together, which was something she could never have managed alone so soon, and by the time Kyle had entered her life the 'Briony H' label was one year and two collections old, had a foot in the UK market and the Continent in its sights for the next year. The US after that, was Derek's agenda. Derek's ambition more than matched her own, the difference between them being that she wanted the challenge and fulfilment of a successful career, while Derek wanted the kudos, and the money.

Their personal relationship had stayed amicable and they continued to go to the odd party together, which was how she had come to meet Kyle at 'a publishing do in Holland Park that's worth attending for a bit of networking,' as Derek had described it.

Leaving Derek busily 'networking', Briony had wandered out to the conservatory to get away from the crush. A glass of wine in her hand, she had stood among the plants, looking out through the glass wall at the reddish smoggy night sky of London.

'The sky is black where I come from and you couldn't put a pin between the stars.' The voice was right behind her and she spun around, into him, the movement sending some of her wine splashing to the floor.

'I didn't mean to startle you. I thought you knew I'd followed you out.' He didn't smile with the apology — not apology, explanation.

A hard, sculpted kind of face. . .had been her first impression when she had seen him earlier in the evening, and then hadn't been able to keep her eyes from straying to him, seeking him out across the room and finding his own eyes waiting to meet hers. Close up, the impression of hardness was reinforced, of planes and angles, and bones that might have had a fineness about them, but no softness. The nose was strong and prominent, the eyes deep-set under the heavy sweep of black brows. They stayed unwaveringly on her face. 'I've been watching you all evening. I thought you knew that too.'

He was in a dark suit, and, except for the pale skin and white shirt, everything else about him was dark—black hair, eyes. . .clothes, and the dramatic effect of him heightened by the dimness of the conservatory and by an intensity in him—about him—which Briony felt was somehow threatening, and, at the same time, dangerously attractive.

'Yes,' she admitted with no thought of putting on a pretence that she had not noticed him watching her, but with a curious little thrill that he had been as drawn to her as she to him.

His smile at her frank admission was a slow, sensuous curve of the lips, and in that moment something passed between them as they locked eyes, and she was lost, to Kyle Buchanan, whose agent had organised the party to celebrate the signing up of his book for a TV series in America. Years later, Briony still couldn't explain, understand, what it was that had drawn them together so instinctively.

They stayed in the conservatory for the rest of the evening, talking of things people didn't usually talk about at parties. . .of Vikings, she remembered vividly, and of ancient Scottish clans. They could have talked of train timetables and she would have been equally enthralled. They had danced too, moving languidly in between the ferns and flowers to music drifting in to them from the party, and the effect of his body against her body was like a sudden gale bringing a calm sea to surging turbulence. Going on twenty-three, she had never been to bed with any man, yet she would have gone to bed with Kyle that night if he'd wanted her to.

Kyle had other plans.

The party had been on a Saturday, and during the following week they were with each other every evening, on strangely conventional dates in public places. . .the theatre, a concert. . .dinners, when all she wanted was for them to be alone. As Kyle wanted too, yet deliberately held off from what they both knew was inevitable. She sensed the tension in him . . .the suppressed passion that threatened to unleash itself in his goodnight kisses, which were the only physical contact he allowed between them during that week.

The next Saturday morning he arrived at her flat unexpectedly and very early, and ordered her to put on something comfortable and very warm. He himself was in a navy jersey with a dark, heavy jacket over dark trousers, and, although she didn't realise it at the time, it was the Kyle of Barra who had materialised that Saturday morning. To take her to his island, he told her.

They reached Barra mid-afternoon, with Heathrow, Glasgow and a petrifying flight over a raging Minch behind them. It was early December and Barra was already in cold, cloudless dusk, the wind wild, the hills black and bleak, and Reef House like a brooding sentinel beside the turbulent water.

'This is where I live, I want you to live here with me.'

Kyle had meant marry him first, she learnt later.

The crashing of a wild sea was background to her own wild cries of ecstasy when Kyle made love to her that night when the sky was as black as he had said it was, and so thick with stars that they looked like a trail of silver silk across the blackness through the window. It was exquisitely tender love, Kyle knowing without being told that it was her first time, and he seemed unsurprised, almost as if he had expected that that was the way it would be — that he would be her first and only lover. His own cries came in a language Briony had never heard before. '*Tha gaol agam ort. Is tu mo ghràdh. M'eudail.*'

'I love you. You are my love. My darling,' were the first Gaelic words she learnt.

Kyle made love to her all week, or so her recollection had it, before they returned to London to be married six weeks later.

If Kyle had had his way they would never have left the island. And neither would she, if she had the choice again.

CHAPTER TWO

BRIONY's half-hope — that whoever turned up with the cab wouldn't recognise her — sank at the sight of the nuggety little figure of Jimmy MacTaggerty, one of Kyle's neighbours, climbing out of the cab.

'*Tha I breagh an diugh.* Och, and what a grand sight it is to see you back, Mrs Buchanan.' The weatherbeaten face shone with pleasure in the ear-to-ear beam.

The Gaelic caught her unprepared. 'Yes, it is beautiful,' Briony returned after a moment, and gave a laugh — a spontaneously happy sound she had not heard from herself for months, at having managed to translate Jimmy's 'It's a beautiful day today' — the mandatory comment on the weather which nearly always preceded local conversation, the 'beautiful,' in this case, applying to the pale sunshine bathing the sun-starved little island.

'Just testing that the Gaelic has not deserted you,' Jimmy grinned, and Briony felt some of her tension leave her as Jimmy chatted them into his cab as if she had never been away. 'Reef House, is it now?'

'No, Jimmy, not for the moment. I need to go into Castlebay first,' Briony told him hastily, and was relieved that he didn't seem to find anything odd in that, but instantly began to fill her in on every birth, marriage and death since her last visit, taking it for granted that she was interested. And she was — or

26

would have been, if it were not for more pressing things on her mind.

'Now look at that; it's behind the hill fences they should be this time of year,' Jimmy growled in annoyance at the five sheep strolling unperturbed too close to the edge of the narrow, winding road, the coloured patches of identification on their backs making them look like a row of woolly flags on the move. He edged past them with such a malevolent hiss out of the window that Briony couldn't restrain a chuckle.

Everything was so endearingly familiar. . . Jimmy, the colour-patched sheep taking right of way. . .the small cottages of intermittent villages and croft holdings beside the road which had starkly towering hills on the one side of it, and dark green waters dotted with islands large and small on the other. Familiar and loved, not just because this was Kyle's island and she loved him, but because it always felt like coming home. Knowing that this would be her last time here made the sense of familiarity all the more poignant.

From the Traigh Mhor in the north it was approximately seven miles to Castlebay in the south whether you went by the east or the west side of the island. Jimmy had taken the east side — Kyle's side, with the hills more brooding even in the fragile sunlight, the slopes rockier, and with no sweeps of green machair running gently to the water's edge as they did on the west. As they passed the turn-off to Kyle's house, Briony stared straight ahead.

'And here we are already, Bagh a Chaisteil,' Jimmy announced when Castlebay lay like a picture postcard beneath them as they cruised down the last slope into the 'town', with its castle in the sea, and one tiny main street, known simply as the Street. 'I've some things to attend to myself, Mrs. Buchanan, but will be through in half an hour, and if you can wait I'll be happy to take you on home,' Jimmy offered as he pulled up in the car park-cum-town square at the top of the Street.

'Thank you. I just need to go to the post office, then I'll have a cup of tea and wait for you.'

She didn't need to go to the post office, nor to have come into Castlebay at all. It had been an excuse to get away from Kyle, if only temporarily, and, while at the back of her mind there had been the flicker of intention to try and find accommodation through the Tourist Office, Briony had abandoned it. Even an out-of-the-way B and B on, say, Vatersay, the small island connected to the south end of Barra by a causeway, was out of the question. A two-week stay while Kyle was away from the island would have been a different matter; people would have assumed that she didn't want the inconvenience of opening up the large house, whereas a three-day stay, with Kyle in residence at Reef House, would be fraught with embarrassment for everybody, not least herself, if she went around asking after accommodation. Not to mention having to face Kyle's wrath afterwards.

Leaving the suitcase in the cab, Briony made good her lie by going to buy some stamps, then, recognised and greeted by surprised smiles and, 'Welcome back, Mrs Buchanan,' she walked back up the Street, and past the little square to trek up the steep flight of

steps to the hotel perched on the hill alongside the
church. After the confrontation with Kyle, it was a
drink she needed, rather than a cup of tea. She went
into the bar, ordered a gin and tonic, then brought it
out to one of the tables on the veranda and gazed
down at Kisimul Castle standing solidly in the bay
which looked more like a large lake with the slopes
of Vatersay extending the slopes of Barra itself into
almost a ring around the water. From where she sat
she could also see the tiny main street, curving
around to the pier, and, beyond the roofs directly
below her, dozens of boats adding to the scene which
never failed to take her breath away.

'Admiring the view?'

Briony turned to the stocky, sandy-haired man
who had followed her out of the bar, a beer in his
hand. 'Yes,' she replied shortly, but with a smile
taking the edge off the abruptness.

'You must be a visitor since I haven't seen you
around before, and I flatter myself I can now tell
locals and visitors apart. I'm Martin Gunn. May I
join you?'

'Briony Hayward. Yes, do.' Briony gestured
towards the vacant chair. 'And yes,' she continued
as he settled himself beside her, 'I've just come in on
this afternoon's plane from Lewis—only for a few
days,' she pre-empted the next question. 'I take it
you're not a visitor yourself?' she asked, mildly
curious. His accent was Scottish but of the mainland,
the clothes casual, and, while he didn't look local, he
didn't look like a tourist either.

'Oh, I like to think I've progressed beyond the
visitor stage,' he laughed. 'I've been here four

months now and will be around for another six yet. I'm the consultant architect for the new housing project on Vatersay and have rented a house there until Christmas. Where are you staying?'

Briony hesitated, and, in the pause, the solution to all her problems streaked into her mind from nowhere. Not exactly from nowhere, from the sudden recollection of Jimmy's mention that Kyle's old gillie, Shonny, had died some months ago. 'In a cottage on the Reef House estate,' she said offhandedly.

'Reef House? That's Kyle Buchanan's place, isn't it?'

'Yes, I believe it is,' she agreed, vaguely.

Martin looked puzzled. 'I didn't know he'd taken to letting cottages.'

Neither did Kyle; Briony almost laughed.

'I don't know him or anything,' Martin put in hastily. 'Just on nodding terms, and I suspect he nods to everybody. It's. . .well, it's rather hard to get to know the locals,' he confided with a rueful grin.

To be accepted by the locals, Briony knew he meant, and that was true, and if she herself had been so readily accepted it was only because she was Kyle's wife, and Kyle was one of them. She finished her drink and stood up. 'I must go. That's my cab driver heading towards his cab down there. Nice to have met you Martin.' Briony started to move away from the table.

Martin had stood up too. 'What are you doing this evening?' he asked, almost brusque in his shyness, and after another quick glance at her ring — white-gold twists of ancient Celtic knots, but unrecognisable as the wedding-ring it was. Reassured, he hurried on. 'I mean, if you've no other plans you might like to join me for dinner this evening.'

Briony looked back at him in surprise. It might be hard to be accepted by the locals, but girls were girls anywhere, and she would have thought that a pleasant-looking, unattached chap like Martin should not have had too much trouble attracting feminine interest.

'That's very nice of you, Martin, but no, thank you. I'm awfully tired after all the travelling today.' She softened the rejection with a warm smile. 'But I'll probably see you around,' she added, because on an island that was five miles by eight everybody ran into everybody sooner than later.

She hurried down the steps, unnecessarily, since Jimmy was chatting by the car and looking in no hurry to go anywhere. Island time ran to its own, very special clock, and on each visit it had always taken her a while to get used to the unhurried pace, only to have trouble adjusting to London's every-minute-counts pace, on her return there.

'Reef House it is, Mrs Buchanan.'

It wasn't a question — for either of them. 'Yes, thank you, Jimmy.' Briony felt the tension springing back, and then heightening with each mile closer to Kyle.

Midway between the airport and the town, Reef House was reached by a stony drive which started at the main road and meandered around and between the outcrops of rocks along a flattish stretch of ground before dipping quite sharply towards the water. The large two-storeyed house — three-storey counting the attics — was half-way down the slope and facing the sea and reefs which gave it its name. It had passed to Kyle upon his widowed mother's marriage to an American businessman and her subsequent move to the US about ten years ago, and by mainland standards Reef House, or Taigh na Sgeire — House of Reef, as it was in the Gaelic — was isolation personified. Yet Kyle's old family home was no more remote than a lot of other houses on the island, and its remoteness was one of the things Briony had really loved when Kyle had first brought her here, when she and Kyle had been so much in love, and Reef House their private magical retreat from the world. It wasn't any more and the prospect of having to stay there among all the memories was unbearable — whatever Kyle expected, she was not going to subject herself to that.

Jimmy bumped them over the last bit of drive, pulling up at the side of the grey solid stone house in the same moment as Kyle came out of the porch, the timing too neat to be coincidence and giving the impression that he had been on the look-out for her. Another time it would have been because he couldn't wait for her to come; now Briony knew it was only because he hadn't trusted her to turn up as ordered.

She stood by without protest while he paid Jimmy off. Objecting to her husband seeing to her fare would have looked odd to Jimmy, besides which, Kyle would have been furious if she'd initiated an argument in front of the cab driver, and she didn't want an angry, intransigent Kyle for what she had to tell him.

'I'm not staying, Kyle,' Briony blurted nervously

after Jimmy had handed her suitcase to Kyle and was safely out of earshot in his cab. 'I mean not in the house,' she qualified hastily as Kyle's eyes flashed. 'I've decided I'd prefer to stay in the cottage and——'

'I think that's something we'd better discuss inside.' Kyle simply went on ahead into the house, leaving her no option but to follow him. He put the case down just inside the hall and turned to her. 'Welcome home.'

The irony was predictable but disturbing none the less, and Kyle's smile even more so; it didn't reach his eyes and their dark Celtic blue looked threateningly black in the shadowy light of the hall.

Briony shook her head agitatedly, rattled by the irony, by Kyle's soft, sardonic smile, and most of all at finding herself where she had never expected to be again—under her husband's roof, where Kyle didn't want her, any more than she wanted to be there.

'Please, Kyle, don't make it difficult for me. I *can't* stay here.' She was appalled to hear the pleading in her voice. 'I won't stay here.' The attempt at firmness came over as stubbornness. Kyle's jaw tightened. 'It can't make any difference to you if I stay in the cottage, can it?'

'Other than the disappointment of being deprived of your company, no,' Kyle conceded with mocking regret, yet not vetoing the cottage outright, Briony noted, and determinedly ignored the mockery.

'I'll be quite comfortable in Shonny's. I. . . Jimmy mentioned that he died recently. I'm sorry,' she added, knowing how fond Kyle had been of the eccentric old man who had looked after the property's sheep and who had entertained her on numerous occasions with wonderful tales of Barra's past, the more improbable ones always preceded by Shonny's deadpan, 'Now this is true, lass.'

Kyle acknowledged the condolence with a shrug, then studied her pensively for a long monent. 'Do you find the prospect of staying here so unacceptable? Really. . .? You surprise me, Briony,' he went on when she returned the tiny jerky nod. 'I'd have thought that, whatever your feelings towards me, you'd still have preferred the comforts of your own house.' The brief gesture of his hand encompassed the hall, a room in itself, and in the mornings quite beautiful with the sunlight streaming in through the window in the wall beyond the staircase. In very late afternoon, as it was now, the tapestries and paintings hung darkly from their walls and no light gleamed off the polished wooden floor, or caught the colours of the flowers on the small round table near the foot of the stairs. Briony remembered an elderly lady in the village down the road once telling her that this was the dark side of the island, and that was the way it felt now inside Kyle's hall. . . Kyle's house — shadowy. . .brooding, with the dark figure of Kyle himself adding to the threatening air that Briony's strained nerves were projecting all over the place.

She was shaking her head as she returned her eyes to him. 'No, Kyle, yours, not mine, and you can't force me to stay here,' she put in on a spurt of desperate defiance.

'*Force* you, Briony?' Kyle repeated the word with distaste. 'And just when have I ever attempted to force you into anything you didn't wish to do? Never, to my recollection, and I certainly have no intention of attempting to start now,' he assured her coldly. 'So what do you propose to do? Cart yourself and your suitcase the odd half-mile down a couple of sheep tracks. . .? Or did you have in mind that I would play bellhop for you?'

'I. . .'

'Exactly. You haven't thought the ridiculous notion through at all.'

Kyle was right; in her desperation to get there, she had not given a thought to the mechanics of reaching the cottage, but that was the least of her problems now that she knew Kyle did not intend to prevent her going. 'I wouldn't dream of inconveniencing you and am perfectly capable of getting myself there, thank you.'

'I don't doubt you are.' Kyle jerked his lip in an unamused smile. 'However, I'd prefer that my wife didn't make a spectacle of herself frantically hauling her case over the hills like some Victorian scullery maid in flight. If you're so keen on the cottage, then Neil shall take you there.'

'Oh, but——'

Kyle left the hall without waiting to hear the end of the protest. Briony stayed, relieved, yet puzzled too. Kyle had been reasonable, not intransigent as she had feared, and letting her have her way with almost an indifference to what she did or where she stayed, so long as it was on his property. He hadn't even asked why she had returned to Barra. Did he think it was to attempt a last-ditch reconciliation, and was he telling her, without actually saying it, that since she had rejected his ultimatum to return in March it was too late now for her to make any such move. . .? But she knew that herself, and if there had been any lingering hopes, then four months of silence from Kyle had managed to crush them.

'Neil will take you now.' Kyle had returned with his estate manager at his side.

'Hello, Neil.' Briony gave him a quick, uncomfortable smile.

'Mrs Buchanan,' Neil acknowledged her with a nod and no hint of his usual pleasure at seeing her. Like Morag, Kyle's housekeeper, he had been part of the household since Kyle's mother's day, and, like the housekeeper, he was devoted to Kyle. He was a discreet man, but from the closed-up, unhappy look on his face it was obvious that at this moment he was also a very embarrassed man, while from the hard, grim set of Kyle's face, it was obvious that *he* was furious at having been forced to draw his employee into his private affairs.

'I'm sorry,' she murmured to Kyle. 'For the inconvenience.' And the embarrassment, she meant, which she had not foreseen and very much regretted. 'If I could just have the key I won't trouble you any longer.'

'Key?' Kyle repeated, then his face cleared. 'I think you'll find you'll be able to let yourself in without one. You've been away too long, Briony, and seem to have forgotten that we don't go in for things like that here,' he reminded her sarcastically. 'Thank you, Neil.' With a nod that dismissed both her and Neil, Kyle turned his rigidly angry back on them and disappeared into the corridor leading off the hall.

Neil picked up the suitcase and led the way out of the house and around the side of it to Kyle's estate car. He made no comment about her destination, or about anything at all, as he drove them up the stony drive in embarrassed silence. About two hundred yards from the house, he turned into a narrow track that bumped the car over still stonier ground for a quarter of a mile or so, then came to an abrupt stop. No car could go further. The cottage was another quarter of a mile down a rocky incline and almost at the water's edge, and reached only by a path Shonny and his sheep had beaten over the years.

Her suitcase in hand, Neil started down the path in the same strained silence and Briony followed, picking her way over the stones and boggy bits of ground along the track to the old stone cottage where the door swinging on its hinges instantly explained Kyle's reassurance that she wouldn't need a key, but didn't prepare her for the horror when she stepped inside.

Neil placed the case on the floor that seemed to consist mainly of gaps in between a few floorboards and looked at her expectantly while Briony tried to keep the horror from showing on her face. He appeared to be waiting for her to say something. Something like, I can't stay here; take me back please. . .?

'Thank you, Neil. I'll be fine now,' she said stiffly, and felt awful when she saw the worry in his eyes. 'You go back now. I'll be fine,' she repeated firmly, and then had to stop herself from running out after him and telling him that she had changed her mind, and that she couldn't stay in this hideous place.

An original croft cottage from the last century, it was a one-room affair—what was left of it—and, while Shonny had died only two months ago, he must have moved from the dank, filthy place long before that, because with part of the roof gone, the glass out of the windows, it was clear that the cottage had not been inhabited for ages and was being readied for complete restoration. Kyle's reasonableness was no longer puzzling, and it hadn't been reasonableness but malice that had been behind his too-ready agreement to her coming here, knowing that she would have to return to Reef House once she saw the state of the cottage.

Over the first shock, Briony took a second look at the appalling sight, focusing on the dilapidated table and chair still by the blackened fireplace which Shonny had fed with peat all year round. Other than a pile of old lobster crates in one corner, the table and chair were the only pieces of 'furniture'. She studied the chair thoughtfully. If she covered it with her mac from the suitcase, she could possibly, just possibly, sit out a night.

One night. To make at least a token gesture of protest against being used to keep up appearances at Reef House. And then pay for that one night of defiance with two miserable days of Kyle's icy anger. . .?

Perhaps that was what her hurt needed: Kyle at his worst to take away the memories of Kyle at his best. . .loving, passionate. . .supportive—all the things he had been when he had uprooted himself

from Barra for the sake of her career and her
business with Derek, whom he disliked thoroughly,
and vice versa.

London for two years had been their agreement,
by which time the 'Briony H' label should have gone
into the US. Should have, but hadn't, and the two
years had stretched into two and a half before they
had finally made the move to Barra last July, but
with Briony still as determined as Derek to capture
the elusive US market, wanting that last boost to her
reputation before setting up to freelance from Barra,
hundreds of miles from the nearest fashion centre.

It had meant flying back to London for weeks at a
time, an arrangement Kyle had hated as much as she
had and both knew couldn't last. At the end of
September, after barely two months of 'commuting',
Briony had returned to their Kensington apartment.
For six months, then, US or no US, the partnership
would be over and she would start freelancing, she
had promised Kyle, who had reluctantly accepted
the new arrangement and taken on the travelling
himself, flying down to London fortnightly in
between the long-distance phone calls which cost
them a fortune, and the only thing that had made the
strain bearable was the knowledge that it would all
be over by the end of March —— And would have
been if Derek hadn't sprung the new project on her
in early February, contracted the business — her — to
a one-off collection for Japan which would have to
keep her in London until the end of June. Briony
had been appalled and furious.

'But it's you they're clamouring for, Briony, and
isn't that what you want?' Derek countered when

she told him to find another designer. 'I'd have thought you'd be over the moon. I'm sure Kyle will understand once you've explained we're legally contracted to come up with the collection.' Derek played his ace smugly.

Hating the thought of Kyle's disappointment, of imposing another three months of travelling on him, Briony had put off the inevitable discussion week after week, and as her own tension mounted she had sensed a corresponding tension in Kyle. In the end, and only two weeks before the end of March, Kyle had found out, in the worst possible way.

Derek had just brought her home from a fashion function they'd had to attend together and was about to leave when Kyle turned up, a day earlier than expected.

'Hello, old chap; Briony didn't tell me you were due from the Hebridean wilds.' Derek put on a show of surprised delight.

'Saunders,' Kyle acknowledged him frigidly, and, to Briony's shock, included her in the same icy look and did not come to take her into his arms as he always did. 'Am I interrupting something?' The thin, deadly smile sent her into a freeze.

'Not at all. Come and make yourself at home. Can I get you a drink?' Derek offered with a bray of a laugh but, despite the blasé air, Briony could tell he was intimidated by Kyle's suppressed anger.

'I am at home and quite capable of pouring myself a drink in my own house if and when I choose,' Kyle returned through his teeth. 'You were just leaving, Saunders. . .?'

The hostility between the two men had never been

more open and Derek was heading towards the door as he spoke. 'Yes, well, I will push off if you don't mind.' He turned to Kyle from the door. 'Oh, and thanks for letting me keep Briony from you for another couple of months. Oops, have I let the cat out of the bag?' He grinned malice into her appalled face, then switched the grin to Kyle's stony mask. 'I thought you already knew, since it was all fixed up at least six weeks ago—the extra collection Briony has promised to do for me. All part of a legally binding contract, by the way,' he added before letting himself out, unnoticed by Kyle, who had not taken his eyes off her.

'I didn't agree to it. I mean, not in the beginning. I'd never have done that without talking to you first,' Briony launched guiltily into the long-overdue explanation.

'So you agreed to whatever it was six weeks ago?' Kyle ignored the explanation; he was nodding slowly, and seemed unsurprised. 'Yes, I see.'

'Not agreed, had no choice,' she corrected heatedly.

'No choice but to keep it from me? To lie to me about returning to Barra?'

'Lie?' The accusation shocked her into an involuntary laugh. 'I didn't lie to you, Kyle; how can you even think it? I. . . I just didn't know how to tell you that I can't leave London until the end of June.'

'Can't or won't, Briony?' Kyle shot at her so nastily that she was taken aback. 'Are you sure that you really want to leave? Or that Derek will let you?'

'Of course I want to leave, and it's not up to

Derek. It's only that he's contracted me to the new collection and I have to do it because——'

'Then you can do it from Barra,' Kyle cut her off sharply. 'Yes, Briony,' he insisted as she shook her head. 'I want you to start working from the island as we agreed, and you can start with your—his— wretched collection.'

'But you don't understand; it's just not possible with this Japanese one. I need to be on the spot to organise the fabrics, the pattern-making and—— It would only be for another three months, Kyle.' Briony stopped the frustated explaining and resorted to pleading.

'And then another three for another collection. . .?' Kyle challenged in soft anger. 'No, *m'eu-dail*. I'm not giving you any more time. I've made all the compromises I'm going to make—too many of them, if anything—and I'm not prepared to make any more. As far as I'm concerned it's come to either or: return to Barra with me now or don't return at all. And I mean now, Briony; I'm foreclosing even on the two weeks that are left to the end of the month.'

Kyle was intransigent and they had fought as they had never fought before with neither giving an inch, and then somehow ended up making love with a passion that was almost savage. Afterwards, Briony had thought they had made up, until she realised that Kyle did not intend to stay the night.

They had not been making up. In stunned disbelief she had watched him walk out—out of their marriage, as it turned out, and if she had realised that then she would have dropped everything, risked Derek suing her for her last penny, and flown to

Kyle. Yet in spite of the furious row, in spite of his ultimatum, she had not really believed that Kyle had been serious until she had tried to telephone him the next week to let him know she needed to go to Paris for a few days so that she and Derek could finalise a 'manufacture under licence' contract with a firm wanting to produce their label in France. Expecting Kyle to have cooled down, she had also wanted to talk calmly about their impasse, which she had assumed to be temporary.

She hadn't got a chance to talk to him about anything. Kyle was out of the country, was the information she had received from Reef House, and couldn't believe it — that Kyle would go anywhere without telling her — but, whether he had really been away or simply refusing to take her calls, she could not reach him and the messages she had left on Barra and in London had brought no acknowledgement. Nor had the desperate letters she had added to the phone calls over the weeks that followed.

Six weeks of silence from Kyle had finally brought home just how serious he had been, and shocked, hurt, Briony had given up trying to contact him, abandoned all thought of a frantic flight to Barra and tried to immerse herself in her work, taking on the Hebridean Collection after the Japanese one because there was no reason not to. She still intended to sever the partnership but it would be in her own time now, she had decided angrily, and was surprised how much anger had settled in underneath the hurt. A dull, deep anger that Kyle had rejected all her efforts towards reconciliation. . .that he had let their marriage end so quickly and so unequivocally. As if he had wanted it to end. And perhaps he had.

Because of beautiful Ishabel waiting in the wings on Barra. . .? Or was her imagination beginning to run away with her in the ghastly surroundings? Briony wondered miserably as she went outside to walk down the slope to the water just to get away from the unspeakableness inside the cottage.

It was cold by the water, the wind whipping bitingly off the sea, and, while the long summer twilights didn't really turn into blackness this far north, the ominously darkened, downpour-threatening sky made it seem much later than it actually was. She peered at her watch and couldn't believe it was only nine, only three hours since Neil had left her, and an endless freezing night ahead unless she started back to Reef House immediately. In the face of the coming storm the humiliating return was inevitable, and she must have been mad even to have contemplated freezing to death in a foul cottage on the edge of nowhere when half a mile away there was warmth, food and a bed waiting for her. And Kyle's malicious amusement. . .? Or still the same steely anger as when he had ordered Neil to bring her here? Whichever it was, she would have to face it.

Shivering, and suddenly really alarmed by the black skies, Briony hurried back to change out of the light linen outfit into something warm from the suitcase before she abandoned the case and set off. The cottage was in darkness and it seemed colder inside than out, with the wind howling through every gap in the roof and floor, and whistling down the chimney and in through the glassless windows. Her hands ice, she fumbled the key out of her purse and was feeling for the lock when the tiny key slipped out of her numbed fingers. With a yelp of dismay, she dropped to her knees beside the case and frantically ran her hand over the rough floorboards, felt the blast of air up through the large gap, and realised where the key had gone.

Her laugh sounded hysterical to her own ears as she clambered to her feet in the same moment as the water hit her from above, and when she tried to move out of range of it the rain hurled itself at her through the windows, the open doorway; every step she took was into more wetness than she was trying to escape until she stumbled her way into the corner with the crates and found what seemed to be the one dry spot in the entire cottage.

Teeth chattering, and shivering uncontrollably, she gingerly sat down on one of the boxes, hugging herself in the clinging wet linen in a futile attempt to stay warm. 'Welcome back to Barra.' She tried for irony to fight back the tears of sheer misery threatening to overwhelm her at the realisation that she was likely to be trapped in the cottage for hours — or the whole night if Barra's sudden summer storm followed its predictable pattern.

The shaft of light outside the window was lightning, Briony assured herself, then, as her precarious nerves gave way, all of old Shonny's ghostly stories of mysterious lights and unearthly manifestations rushed into her mind together with the irrational panic, and when first one light, and then a second, flashed into the cottage itself she would have screamed if she'd found her voice.

'Briony!' Kyle's voice was harsh with concern. 'Briony. . .? Where——? Oh, God.' His torchlight flashed on to her panic-stricken face and then off it to the floor, to guide his way across the room. Reaching her, he put the torch on the floor and, hauling her up off the crate, immediately began to bundle her into a weatherproof jacket. 'Everything is all right, Neil. Get yourself back to the car.' The concern was gone so quickly from Kyle's voice that it might never have been there.

Neil here too. . .? Briony came out of her fright not into relief, but into a blur of mortification that, because of her, Neil had been dragged out into the storm by a furious Kyle. He was so furious that her arms felt wrenched out of their sockets as Kyle rammed them into the sleeves of the jacket in a silence that was worse than any unleashed anger, which she deserved and would have preferred to the seething hostility radiating at her from the dark oilskin-clad body and ungentle hands pulling the hood of the jacket over her streaming hair.

'Leave the case for tomorrow, Neil,' Kyle called out at the sound of heavy dragging along the floor. Finished with yanking up the jacket zip, he picked up the torch, put a hard, crushing arm around her shoulder, and manoeuvred her towards the door.

'I can manage the case OK.' Neil's disembodied voice came from near the light flashing by the fireplace.

'I couldn't get it open—the case. The key went through the floorboards,' Briony chattered through her teeth. 'That's why I'm wet and—— My handbag!' Inanely, she tried to turn back for it before Kyle had quite pushed her out into the obliterating rain and a wind that made her gasp with shock.

'I've got that too, Mrs Buchanan,' Neil said from somewhere behind her, calmly, soothingly, in contrast to Kyle's harsh mutter, of which she only caught the words 'crazy idiot'.

With the arm around her locking her into his side and lifting her half off her feet, Kyle propelled her up the slope, scooping her bodily into his arms for the last stretch of path and depositing her into the back seat of the car as if she'd been a child snatched out of the rain. Climbing in beside her, he switched on the ceiling light for the short wait for Neil, and in the light Briony risked her first look at his face, white and set into such jagged fury under the wet black hair that the apology she'd been about to attempt stopped dead on the tip of her tongue. She swung her face from him and, edging into the corner of the seat, slumped into a miserable shivering silence until Neil finished putting her case into the back and flung himself into the driver's seat. Like Kyle, he was in a black oilskin, and, like Kyle, he didn't say a word.

Unable to stand the men's grim silence any longer, Briony started talking—babbling, again, about the key going through the floor, and that she would have been OK if she had managed to get her mac out of the case. She was still talking, possibly incoherently, when Kyle got her into the hall and all the while he was whipping the dripping jacket off her to throw on to the floor where he had tossed his own.

CHAPTER THREE

'I'LL only say this once, Briony. Please do not mention that wretched case again. In fact you'd do me a favour by not speaking at all,' Kyle ground out through his teeth, then wound his arm around her again and half carried her up the stairs and along the first-floor landing to the room at the end of it. Their bedroom; Kyle's bedroom now and the last room in the house she wanted to set foot in.

'Oh, no, Kyle, not in here. I don't——'

Ignoring her protest, Kyle left her standing just inside the door and headed out of the room, returning a moment later with two towels from the bathroom next door. Tossing one on to the bed, he wrapped the other around her wet hair, then moved her closer to the fireplace and the fierce heat which was radiating from the peat and filling the large room with warmth.

'No, Kyle, I can manage myself,' Briony cried out in fresh protest and tried to back away from him when he caught hold of the edges of the sodden linen jacket.

His face stony, and ignoring the new protest as he had the last, Kyle tugged her out of the jacket and dropped it to the floor without a glance, and without looking at her. The dark, angry eyes were looking past her—or through her, it felt to Briony—and there was something so coldly impersonal in Kyle's movements that she did not immediately react when he reached both hands around her waist and drew her against himself.

It was not an embrace. He was about to undress her — was undressing her, and in a belated reaction her body was shocked into a tremor that had nothing to do with the earlier shivering which had eased off in the warmth of the hall. Her first thought was that she should stop the efficient fingers pulling the zip at the back of her skirt. But she didn't want to stop him, Briony acknowledged to herself while the rational part of her mind was appalled by the desperate need in her that could make her want Kyle's touch, no matter how impersonal, on her body. Hardly breathing, she stood immobile, fighting the urge to put her own arms around him and beg him to take her into his arms, not to make love to her but just to hold her, comfort her, and tell her that somehow everything was going to be all right between them again.

Kyle's eyes swept suddenly to her face. Had he guessed what was going on in her mind. . .? Had her body given her away? As their eyes locked, Kyle's hands stopped in their slide over the curve of her hips; the next moment he all but snatched them away from her, spun on his heel and strode out of the room. The skirt halfway down her hips, Briony stared after him, as mortified as if she had actually voiced every desperate thought that had been going through her mind.

'Go in there now, please, Morag,' she heard him say tersely to the housekeeper, who must have been hovering on the landing because she was in the room almost before Kyle had finished speaking.

Her wrinkled face as much frightened as worried, Morag came flying up to her, a tiny wiry old lady looking swamped by the woolly grey dressing-gown.

'Hello, Morag.' Briony tried to smile and failed dismally.

'Och, lass, what have you been doing to yourself?' Morag enfolded her fiercely in her arms and for a few moments Briony gave in to the need to be comforted, soothed by the murmured Gaelic which she couldn't understand but found reassuring after the tension of Kyle's hostile silence. 'There, there, *m'eudail*, everything will be all right,' Morag kept murmuring as she proceeded to undress and dry her like a child while Briony meekly submitted herself to the kindly fussing. 'Now don't you move from that fire until you're properly warmed,' the housekeeper ordered after she had bundled her into Kyle's dressing-gown over the top of some navy pyjamas from the chest of drawers. 'I only switched on the electric blanket when he went out for you and it won't be warm enough yet.' Morag straightened from picking up the scatter of wet clothes off the floor, and, with the clothes and towels over her arm, shook her grey head, perplexed, but with a bright, angry light in the dark currant eyes. 'The good Lord only knows what got into him—into you both—he taking it into his head to send you to Shonny's like that, and you going. And after he asked me to prepare the room for you this afternoon, and me thinking. . .' She gave another shake of the head without completing what it was she had thought.

'He didn't send me, Morag,' Briony corrected, defensive of Kyle in the face of the old lady's criticism. 'I wanted to go and he let me, that's all.'

'Then you're each as bad as the other.' Morag darted a disapproving glance at Kyle as he walked in on her comment, a mug of something steaming in his hand.

'Thank you, Morag, I'll take over now.'

'I was just leaving,' Morag returned sharply, unfazed by the ultra-polite dismissal. 'Goodnight, lass.'

'Goodnight, Morag. And thank you, I——' Morag had gone. Briony turned her eyes to Kyle. 'There's no need to put yourself out any longer, Kyle; I'm quite all right now.' Her voice made a lie of her statement. Dropping her gaze, she stared bleakly at the fire.

'Here, drink this.' Kyle pushed the mug into her hand.

Briony took it without meeting his eyes. The liquid was hot and sweet and mainly brandy, which she hated. She pulled back from it with a grimace.

'I know you don't like brandy but it will do you good. Try just a little more,' Kyle encouraged with a kindness that was cancelled in the next breath. 'I don't want an invalid on my hands tomorrow, which is what you'll be if you catch cold.' He took the mug from her when she'd managed two-thirds of its contents and put it on the mantelpiece. 'Come on, into bed now,' he said, unexpectedly gently.

She must have been much more in shock than she realised. How else could she have read what she did into Kyle's words, especially after what had happened before he had ordered Morag into the room? Her face, her eyes, had betrayed her, and there was no way she could take back what Kyle had seen in them.

'No, Briony, I do not intend to join you in bed.' Kyle smiled tightly. 'I haven't yet been reduced to making love to a half-drowned woman in shock, whatever she might think. Or want.' The aside was soft and stinging, and he was already out of the room before its full impact hit home.

Briony was glad to be alone, to get into the enormous, blissfully warm bed and close her eyes — and mind — against Kyle's last taunting smile, and every awful thing that had happened to her since her first sight of him from the plane window. Unsurprisingly, she slept badly and surfaced to sounds that seemed at once strange, and yet familiar. . .cries of seabirds mingling with the distant echoes of cuckoos . . .sheep. . .water over rocks. Then, as her disorientated consciousness added images to the sounds, she remembered where she was and other images floated into her mind, all of them of Kyle, coldly furious. . . taunting. Except when he had sat beside the bed during the night. Briony snapped her eyes open. Kyle with her during the night. . .? She must have dreamt it in the snatches of unsettled sleep in between the waking and crying out. Yet the image persisted, of a dark, brooding figure watching over her by the bed. 'I'm here, *m'eudail*.' Had Kyle said that? It had been Morag who had earlier comforted her with the *m'eudails* — 'darlings' — only Briony could have sworn it was Kyle's voice she was remembering now, imagining it because she would have given anything really to have heard him call her darling again, she supposed sadly, and, moving her head to the window, saw cloudless sunshine in place of the capricious dark skies that had landed her so unceremoniously back under Kyle's roof.

'Good morning, lass.' Morag padded into the room. 'And a beautiful day Barra has turned on for you today.'

Briony doubted it. She sat up against the pillow and gave the housekeeper a small embarrassed smile. 'I'm sorry about last night, Morag.'

Morag's mouth went into a pruny pinch. 'Best we don't say anything more about it. You just lie there and rest and I'll bring you up something to eat soon. It's going on lunchtime and you must be starving.'

'No, I'm not.' Food had been the last thing on her mind yesterday, and, while she hadn't eaten since lunching with Derek in Stornoway, Briony still didn't feel at all hungry. 'What are you doing?' she asked, puzzled by Morag's bobbing up and down between the doorway and the foot of the bed.

'Just taking some of your clothes out of the case.'

'Is my case there. . .? Open?'

'Aye. Mr Kyle brought it up last night.'

So Kyle had come into the room after she had fallen asleep. And stayed. . .? 'Where is he now?' she had to ask, to ensure she wouldn't be caught offguard by Kyle walking in on her here or in the bathroom later, which, like all the other rooms in the house, had no lock.

'Somewhere downstairs,' Morag muttered, still unforgiving of her employer, whom she had nannied long before keeping house for him and whose inter-

mittent flashes of unpredictability did not intimidate
her one iota, Briony suspected, and wished she
herself had managed to develop the same immunity
to the darker side of Kyle's temperament.

She took ages in the bathroom, wallowing in the
luxuriantly hot water, washing her hair and then
staying there to dry it with the drier before putting
on jeans and a white T-shirt and returning barefoot
to the bedroom.

Kyle turned from the window. 'Good morning—
afternoon, rather. How are you feeling?'

The smile and pleasantness of the voice caught her
by surprise. 'Fine. Thank you,' Briony replied after
the slight pause, and, relaxing a little out of her
freeze, came into the room as far as the suitcase.
'Thank you for bringing the case up—and opening
it.'

'Picking locks is one of my lesser known
accomplishments.'

She returned a wary smile at the quip. 'I'm sorry
about yesterday and——' The familiar arch of one
dark brow stopped her apology before it reached its
point—the trouble she had unintentionally caused
everyone.

'And is there any particular aspect of yesterday
that you're singling out for regret?' Kyle prompted
drily, and, of all the humiliating images, her mind
selected their last scene by the fireplace.

Briony felt her face warming. 'I meant the trouble
you unnecessarily put Neil and Morag to by not
telling me about the cottage,' she rallied in self-
defensive attack.

'I?' Kyle affected surprise. 'Don't you mean *you*

caused by digging your heels in and not returning with Neil when you saw the state it was in?'

'Which you should have told me about.'

'And would you have believed me?' Kyle challenged with a dry laugh.

Probably not, Briony had to admit—to herself. She gave a belligerent little lift of her shoulders.

'Exactly.' Kyle read the admission in the shrug. 'So why don't we let the matter drop since I don't imagine you'll want to trade this room for Shonny's tonight?'

'But I don't want to stay here. Not in this room. I mean, it's your room and I don't want to inconvenience you any further. Besides, I'd really prefer one of the guest rooms upstairs. It's such a gorgeous view from there, quite inspiring and. . .' She tailed off the nonsense with a shake of the head.

'You won't be inconveniencing me at all, and I'm sure you'll find the view just as gorgeous from here, and equally inspiring,' Kyle assured her with a suavity that was just this side of sarcasm. 'Besides, it's your room too, and I've always been under the impression that you liked it.'

She loved it. It was a beautiful room, and, like the rest of the house, furnished with lovely antiques collected over generations. A room full of memories. The room in which Kyle had first made love to her, and then made love to her countless times more.

Kyle had been watching her involuntary survey of the room and there was something about the slightly through-the-lashes look that gave her the uneasy feeling that he had been following her train of thought, which was ridiculous. 'Where will you sleep tonight?' she asked abruptly.

'As opposed to where I slept — or rather spent — last night, do you mean?'

He had been with her. She was no longer in doubt about that, yet her mind couldn't adjust to the confusing contrast of a concerned Kyle who had watched over her during the night and the mocking, sarcastic Kyle with her now.

'So where would you like me to sleep, Briony?' he drawled suggestively, the combination of voice and question shooting a shiver down her spine.

Did he expect her to trip herself into a repetition of the embarrassing hopes she had unwittingly revealed to him last night. . .? Briony forced herself to hold his gaze. 'Look, Kyle, last night I didn't mean that I. . .well, that I wanted you to. . .' She couldn't say the 'sleep with me'. 'I didn't come here — to Barra, I mean — thinking that we. . .' He was not making it easier for her with the unwavering gaze trained on her, one brow a fraction higher than the other as he waited to see how she got herself out of the verbal tangle. 'I haven't come looking for a reconciliation,' Briony finally said point-blank.

Kyle's expression didn't change. 'Why have you come back to Barra?'

She had been expecting the overdue question and was prepared for it. 'Work,' she replied flatly, and saw the instant tightening of Kyle's face muscles. 'Derek has come up with the idea of a special winter collection for the US, all in tweeds and cashmere — our Hebridean Collection.' The term tripped off her tongue and sounded awfully twee. 'Derek thinks —

we both think—this will get us into the US market at last and Derek felt it was important for me to refresh my memory of the Hebrides, so to speak, and that I come here straight after visiting the Lewis and Harris mills to make a start on the preliminary sketches.' Dragging Derek's name into every sentence was deliberate and meant to reinforce that it had not been her idea to return to Barra.

Kyle stretched his lips in a tight smile. 'So the partnership still flourishes. For yet another three months, is it? Before you commit yourself to a further three? If you haven't done so already, that is.'

That was how it looked—exactly as Kyle had accused her it would be on the night of their dreadful fight before he had walked out on her. And that was how it was actually turning out, only not because she wanted to continue in the business, but because Kyle had left her with nothing but her career. There was no way she could explain that to him, and she didn't try. 'Anyway, I thought you were in New York, otherwise I'd hardly have turned up to embarrass you, and, since I thought I'd be staying longer, I organised for my car to follow me. I'm afraid it won't be arriving from Stornoway until Wednesday evening so I can't leave until Thursday morning, which means I have no choice but to trespass on your hospitality until then.' She put in the snipe with spurious politeness.

Kyle ignored it. 'Why did you think I was in New York?'

'Derek mentioned something about it,' she muttered offhandedly, in case he thought she had been interested in his whereabouts when she had had to force herself to stop the almost obsessive wondering about his every move before she went mad.

'Ah, yes, of course. A walking, talking mine of information, your Derek — usually.' The voice was loaded with dislike that was borderline venom and the emphasis on the 'your' was curiously overstressed and jarring. 'Where would you be without him?'

The question didn't require an answer. Kyle was just being nasty. Or was he insinuating that she would not have made it as far as she had in her career without Derek as her partner? Work, Derek, both red rags to a bull where Kyle was concerned, and it was she who had unwittingly set the conversation on its hostile course. 'Well, I mustn't take up any more of your time; I'm sure you're very busy.' She changed tack hurriedly and tried to be briskly dismissive. Moving to the dressing-table where her handbag lay on the stool in front of it, she picked up the bag and made out she was about to do something with it, be very busy herself.

Kyle had no intention of being dismissed. Leaning back against the sill of the window, he watched with a faint twist of a smile as she twiddled with the strap of the handbag, and then, as he straightened and came towards her, Briony stopped the twiddling, dropped the bag back on to the stool and began a flustered tucking-in of her T-shirt into the jeans. Then she stopped that too when she realised Kyle was taking in the nervous gesture that could have been construed as a deliberate attempt to draw his attention to her body. She dropped her hands hastily to her sides.

Kyle's eyes travelled slowly back up to her face. 'You've lost weight,' he observed after the appraisal which had seemed quite impersonal yet left her feeling that every stitch of her clothing had been removed along the way. He took another step to close the gap between them, and, putting both his hands to her upper arms, ran them assessingly up and down from her elbow to right up under the sleeve of the top.

She had lost about half a stone since Kyle left her, all of it in those first six weeks after his walk-out, the time it had taken to sink in just how very serious he had been about his ultimatum to her.

Their eyes were almost level; at six-two, Kyle was tall for an islander, while at five-nine she was a tall woman by anybody's standards. Briony looked back into the unreadable dark blue depths, trying not to betray what she felt as he kept stroking her arms. She was not in shock now and her pride, if not her body, rebelled at being deliberately goaded into confirming what she had unintentionally betrayed to him last night.

Her pride, and mind, might have rebelled, but her body was reacting of its own accord to the increasingly sensuous pressure of Kyle's hands, and, as if on cue, the thousand and one tingling nerve-ends were springing to life. Right from the very beginning, Kyle had only had to touch her. . .kiss her. . .brush a hand over her breasts to set off the instantaneous throbbing excitement, and he was too familiar with her body not to know what his touch was doing to her. He had recognised the signs last night and could recognise them now, however hard she fought for control over her reactions. His hands ceased their languid massage and locked tightly around the soft bare flesh of her upper arms.

'But as beautiful as ever,' he murmured huskily, bending his face to her for what was not so much a kiss as soft, sensual contact as Kyle placed his lips over hers and simply held them there for a long, lingering moment before beginning to move his mouth up and down, over and across her lips lightly, then pressing harder but still without any attempt to part her lips. Briony couldn't bear the tantalising teasing any longer; she parted them herself, suddenly offering her mouth to him pleadingly, and felt a tremor through Kyle's body as he finally took possession of her mouth with an unrestrained hunger that matched her own as it had always done in their first breathtaking kiss after any separation.

She tried to lift her hands up to curve tham around his neck but, with Kyle holding her hard by the arms, could only reach them around his waist to draw him closer in her aching need for contact, which, having initiated it, Kyle did not want. Her body had barely brushed against his before he broke off the kiss, released her arms and pulled back from her almost in the same abrupt movement.

'Let's just say that was for old times' sake, shall we?' The long kiss had made his voice slightly breathless, but, breathless or not, it still managed to convey an offhandedness that made her feel mortified.

She spun from him in a haze of humiliation, pushing past him just to get away from him, and found herself at the window where he had stood.

Her back to him, Briony stared blindly at the blur of dark green water beyond the glass. Kyle's eyes were boring—burning into her rigid back. Without seeing them, she could feel them; it felt as if he was still touching her and she hated it.

He had forced her back into his house, and, as if that wasn't enough, had forced her into responses she could no more control than hide from him, only to dismiss them—and his own—with that humiliating 'for old times' sake', which put the kiss into neat, carelessly cruel perspective. As if he had not already made clear that anything and everything between them was in the past—of the past, and that she did not feature in his future.

In London, hundreds of miles away from him, Briony had convinced herself that she had accepted his rejection of her; told herself that surely it was just a matter of another few weeks—a few more months at the most—and she would be over the despair and hurt if only she concentrated on her anger at the way Kyle had walked out of their marriage. Now, after less than twenty-four hours on Barra, she felt catapulted back into those early weeks of hurt and futile hopes, and needs she thought she had managed to suppress but which, it seemed, were still as painfully alive as ever and just waiting to betray her.

Kyle was still there somewhere in the room. 'Leave me alone, Kyle, please,' she ordered wearily, and, turning slowly with the words, saw that he was by the door, his face unreadable as he met her eyes across the room.

'I'll tell Morag you're ready for lunch,' he said brusquely.

A little of her tension went with him. The rest, Briony knew, would be with her until the moment the ferry sailed in two days' time. Two more days . . .of strain, being on guard. . .of keeping her every emotion in check. Of keeping out of Kyle's way and making very sure that she never gave him another chance to break through the protective barrier she was so painfully trying to build around herself, against her feelings for him.

Just the thought of him in the house was enough to make her want to be out of it, and, after the lunch which she insisted on eating in the kitchen with Morag as a safeguard against Kyle finding her alone in the dining-room, Briony put on a navy sweater over the T-shirt, and let herself out of a side-door. She had no destination in mind, her only thought to be away from Kyle.

His car was still where Neil had parked it last night, at the side of the house which gave on to the small flower and vegetable garden, nurtured lovingly by Morag and with a three-sided old dry-stone wall protecting it from the winds. Summer or winter, the winds were part of the island, and the moment she left the windbreak of house and outbuildings Briony was instantly aware of the stiff breeze left in the wake of the night's storm.

Abandoning the futile attempt to restrain her freshly washed hair, she let it fly about unchecked as she clambered over the rocks and followed the sheep-beaten paths up and down and between the slopes the way she and Kyle had used to do for hours—

entire days, sometimes, until she had felt she knew his stark, treeless hills as well as he did. Felt she knew personally the families who had lived in the old cottages that were now only heaps of stones, or a chimney left standing in a crumbling wall — poignant reminders of the often painful past which Kyle had written about in his books. . .told her about, wanting — so passionately — to share his island's past with her. And its future.

They had talked a lot about that — their future — as they had sat here one afternoon on the same large flat stone she was sitting on now, near the remains of one of those ruined cottages in its impromptu garden of wild yellow irises, and with its perennial vista of islands and sea. Later she and Kyle had made love against the very same backdrop of golden irises on that idyllic summer day last July.

Had it been a whole year ago? It must have been, because the Feis had been on then too, and, although they had flown up for it the previous two years, last year had been the first time they had been on the spot for the entire festival. Kyle had taken her to practically everything — concerts, dances. . .the games — a day of exhibitions of Highland dancing, piping, foot races for children and adults alike, and a host of other things. And, besides attending the Feis functions, they'd had people in to dinner. . .gone out to dinner. Briony remembered the two weeks as a wonderful, never-ending whirl of activity, and of wonderful, never-ending lovemaking during those semi-dark summer nights. . .a time of rediscovering each other after the strain of their last months in London before their final move to Barra. And before

the new strain began with the onset of her 'commuting' to London, and, after it, Kyle's 'commuting' to
her.

It had been a mistake to come here, to this place
where they had made love and talked. . .of their
future. . .of starting the family that she had wanted
as much as Kyle. Where they'd been relaxed and
really happy for almost the last time in their
marriage.

Briony sprang up from the stone with a suddenness
that sent a nearby sheep scuttling off in alarm. The
trouble was that every place on the island, every
nook and cranny of it, was associated with Kyle, and
memories which perversely hurt all the more because
they were of times of loving, and of Kyle being
loving. The obvious, sensible thing would have been
to telephone for a cab and have Jimmy drive her into
Castlebay to sit in one of the bustling pubs and be
surrounded by anonymous, cheerful tourists, Briony
realised belatedly as she made her way back to the
house, surprised that it was already going on six.

CHAPTER FOUR

KYLE was coming out of the drawing-room as she let herself into the hall.

'You might have told me you were going out, Briony. I've better things to do than scour three floors looking for you so that Martin Gunn can have the pleasure of speaking to you.'

The name meant nothing. Briony frowned, perplexed, then her face cleared, only to frown again. 'Martin? Did he ring here? But I——'

'Told him not to?' Kyle pounced in with the sarcastic interruption. 'Yes, I'm quite sure you did, but I would have liked you to tell him that again. In my presence.'

So he could play the heavy-handed husband when he no longer had any right to know whom she spoke to or met? 'You surprise me, Kyle.' Briony managed the mock-surprise, prompted by the spurt of anger at his presumption that he could monitor her phone calls. 'I would have thought you'd have spared yourself the scour of the house by reading the riot act to him on the spot.'

Kyle jerked his lips at the rejoinder and put out a very quick hand to clip his fingers around her waist as she tried to go past him to the stairs. 'Believe me, that's exactly what I shall be doing if he ever repeats the mistake of attempting to contact "Ms Hayward" at her husband's house.'

'That's hardly likely, and surely it's obvious that he didn't—doesn't—know that I'm married,' Briony explained with a snap, trying to pick his fingers off her wrist and had to give up in frustration.

Without relaxing his grip, Kyle slid his fingers down to the end of her hand, to lift it up and hold it in almost a parody of their wedding ceremony. 'And surely it's obvious that you're wearing a wedding-ring.' He flicked his eyes to the beautiful twists of white gold, then dropped her hand abruptly. 'My wedding-ring, Briony, and, however inconvenient and temporary our married state might be, while you are still my wife I expect you to behave as my wife. And that means refraining from encouraging the attentions of Martin Gunn or any other man while you are on this island.'

With icy preciseness, Kyle had chosen his words for maximum effect and maximum hurt. Their marriage was a temporary inconvenience—Kyle was spelling it out for her in words that wounded her, just as he meant them to wound; the rest of what he was saying was an insult that made her face flare as furiously as if she had actually been guilty of encouraging Martin as Kyle was insinuating.

'I did not encourage his attentions.' Her voice quavered in angry denial.

'No? Then you shouldn't have put ideas into his head by allowing yourself to be picked up in the first place. Or was it you who did the picking up on the veranda of the pub in Castlebay yesterday?'

'You had me spied on when I went into Castlebay. . .?' Briony stared at him, shocked that Kyle could have stooped to such a thing, yet how else could he have known where she and Martin had met?

Kyle showed his teeth in an angry smile. 'You flatter yourself, Briony, if you think I would waste people's time, let alone my own, in setting anyone to dog your footsteps around this island—a very small island, and if you blatantly select somewhere as public as a pub veranda to initiate acquaintance with men, then as my wife you must expect to be noticed, and for word to get back to me.'

Yes, she should have remembered that, only she had not been doing anything to reflect on Kyle and had had no reason to be devious about a perfectly innocent encounter which she had assumed had ended there and then, whatever Kyle was implying so unfairly, but with no sign of jealousy; it was just appearances that he was so concerned about, and somehow that made his accusation all the more hurtful.

'And how do you know we were just initiating acquaintance and haven't been carrying on in London for yonks?' Briony retorted on a sudden impulse to goad Kyle into showing some sort of emotion apart from the frigidly suppressed anger, and was taken aback by the even colder, more distancing stare.

'Because I know for a fact that your spare time— such as it is—is already accounted for,' he replied icily, and left her staring after him in bewilderment, then at the front door after he had closed it behind him.

In a kind of weary satisfaction, she heard him starting up the car with an angry wrench of the ignition. This was what she had wanted, wasn't it? Kyle at his worst. . .angry, unreasonable, not to mention bewilderingly unfathomable when he threw innuendoes at her that she didn't have a hope of working out.

Her spare time in London accounted for how. . .? In front of the television? Visiting her parents, who had been worried sick about her since Kyle left her? Or attending dreary fashion functions with Derek, who was acting as if the break-up of her marriage was the best thing that had happened to the business as she was now at its disposal twenty-four hours a day to live and breathe the Hebridean Collection as he was doing.

Although it hadn't been her own idea, Briony was the first to admit that it was a wonderful one, prompted, she knew, by Derek's three-day uninvited, unannounced descent on Barra twelve months ago just after she and Kyle had made the move to Reef House. The island he had dismissed, predictably, as 'the end of the earth', and Kyle on his home territory as 'Heathcliff is alive and well and living on Barra', but, for all the sarcasm, a penny had dropped somewhere in Derek's cash register of a brain and had eventually rung up the idea of the Hebridean Collection. If only he had come up with it sooner, then the collection would have been designed, made and shown, the US market theirs, the partnership severed, and her marriage intact. Which would have defeated Derek's purpose in keeping her locked into the business as long as he could, of course, and, even if the idea had actually occurred to him earlier, Briony suspected he would have kept it from her.

That was probably being unfair to Derek, but when had Derek ever been fair to her. . .?

Her aimless wander through the resoundingly empty house had brought her to the kitchen, where she found Morag tidying up.

'I've put out some cold meat in the dining-room but if you'd like something hot I'll stay on and make it for you. I hope you don't mind, but I've arranged for Jimmy to take me over to my daughter Katy's for the evening, not knowing you'd be here, like. Alone, I mean.' Morag darted her an odd glance, almost of embarrassment. 'I could stay, if you'd like me to.'

'Heavens, no.' Briony refused the offer a little sharply. 'Something cold will be fine. You just leave when you're ready.'

'He. . . Mr Kyle has got into the habit of going out most evenings. I'm sorry, lass,' Morag mumbled apologetically, as if it were her fault that her 'Mr Kyle' had acquired this habit. 'I think it's lonely he's become in your absence.' The dark eyes had a rather desperate look in them. . .embarrassment? Sympathy? Morag might as well have said outright that Kyle went off to see Ishabel Macleod every other night.

That was how Briony interpreted the old lady's comment and looks. Her face felt on fire. 'Yes, I believe Kyle did mention something about a previous engagement this evening.' The face-saving fib popped out and made her even more embarrassed — with herself, and later Briony wondered why she had bothered with the pathetic lie when Morag knew exactly the state of her employer's marriage, and, whatever hopes she might have nurtured for their reconciliation, the housekeeper could add up with the best of them, and two and two in Reef House added up to Kyle going his way and Briony hers—

To spend a solitary, miserable evening staring unseeingly at the television in the drawing-room. While Kyle. . .? She didn't want to think about him but he had taken over every corner of her mind, and every thought, whatever it started out as, ended with Kyle as willy-nilly and as obsessively as in those early weeks of his walk-out. The only difference being that there had been no Ishabel Macleod in the pictures her mind had tortured her with then. And now there was.

But she didn't—couldn't know for certain that Kyle was with Ishabel tonight—or any other night, Briony tried to reason, to rationalise away what she recognised as plain simple jealousy—something she had never experienced in her life. Had never had reason to, or so she had thought, naïvely. Or was it arrogantly. . .? She had been so convinced of Kyle's passion for her that the thought of Kyle ever being interested in another woman had never crossed her mind until that shocked moment at the airport when Ishabel had materialised at Kyle's side and looked— behaved as if she had a right to be there. And had been there for how long? wondered Briony drearily as she lay tossing and turning in her bed, listening for sounds of Kyle's return and hearing only the familiar lulling sound of water over reefs until she finally fell asleep.

Kyle was in his study when she came down the next morning to be fussed over by Morag during another solitary meal. Briony didn't want to see him any more than he wanted to see her. . .wasn't up to any more confrontations, innuendoes, or Kyle playing his cruel little games for 'old times' sake'. . .but it was humiliating to be seen to be ignored and be subjected to Morag's sympathetic cosseting as if she were some sort of invalid instead of merely a discarded wife.

He didn't emerge for lunch, and, feeling really unnerved, Briony tapped on the study door at three-thirty to tell him that she was about to go into town to wait for the ferry—it wasn't due for another four hours but she'd sooner be killing time in Castlebay than sitting in the bedroom staring out of the window, riddled with tension just by Kyle's presence in the house, and not up to even the pretence that she was thinking about the designs she had come to commence.

'Yes?' His voice wasn't encouraging.

Briony opened the door and just put her head around it rather than going into the room. 'I'm sorry to disturb you,' she said stiffly.

'You're not. Come in.' Kyle moved the papers in front of him to the side of the desk, a gesture possibly meant to indicate that he was prepared to give her his full attention.

She came a little way into the room, Kyle's very private room, never featured in the 'author at home or work' magazine articles that his agent had sometimes managed to force him into. It was the kind of study people invariably pictured writers working in . . .books lining walls, small stacks of them on side-tables near comfortable leather armchairs in front of the fireplace which Morag had laid with peat in readiness for the changes that Barra's unpredictable summer made a foregone conclusion. Very few writers, however, would have had the magnificent view of rocks and sea and islands that Kyle had from his desk.

'Are you working on a new book already?' she asked politely, to ease her own tension and wave the white flag, signalling that she had not come in for a confrontation. The glance at his desk was one of genuine curiosity, though, because the neat stacks of paper didn't have the usual pages-all-over-the-place look that she had come to associate with Kyle in the early throes of a new book.

He shook his head. 'Only going through some of my old short stories and articles for Henrik — Professor Bergen. I'm picking out the odd one here and there which has any reference to Celtic mythology — stuff I did years ago.'

'Oh, I don't think I've read any of them, have I? I was up until late last night, reading.' Briony horrified herself with the conversational quantum leap and knew what was coming next, but couldn't stop it. 'I didn't hear you come in. Did you have a pleasant evening? With the professor, I suppose. . .?' she tossed in with a glassy-eyed attempt at casualness, and wanted to sink through the floor.

'No, not with the professor. But I did have a pleasant evening all the same, thank you,' Kyle replied, holding her eyes without a blink.

Had she really expected — or wanted — him to confirm that he had been with his girlfriend last night. . .? Or mistress it would be, since on paper at least he was still a married man. Mortified at having been reduced to such desperate prying, Briony swung away from the bland study of her hot face and snatched up the nearest book from the table beside the armchair.

'Haven't you seen it before?'

Kyle's question focused her mind on what her eyes had been staring at—his new book. 'Yes. Yes, I have,' she answered distractedly. 'I picked up a copy in April when it came out.' She had bought it in a bookshop like his other readers instead of reading a proof copy as she had of his second book, which had been published in the first year of their marriage. She had also seen Kyle interviewed about it on a talk show and marvelled that he had appeared so normal . . .so untouched by the break-up of their marriage, when at the end of April she had been at her most devastated. 'I believe it's climbing to number one. Congratulations. It's a great book,' she added, and the sincerity slipped out before she could catch it back.

'I'm flattered you think so.' Kyle smiled drily.

'Oh, I haven't read it, just the reviews. What with one thing and another, I haven't had time for the real thing yet,' Briony lied on the spur of the moment and, as Kyle's smile flicked off, wanted to take back the lie and tell him that yes, of course she had read it, as she had the first two parts of the trilogy that had made him an internationally acclaimed author——

And run the risk of giving away that she had pored over it, through it, time and time again, hearing Kyle's voice in every word, and every word of desperate interest in her insatiable need for contact, if only vicariously, with the man who wrote them?

'I did actually bring a copy along to read on the plane.' She hastily offered the conciliatory lie and realised what an insult it was even as the words left her mouth. Kyle's books were not airport fodder. Intense, absorbing, the trilogy spanned several generations of two families forced out of the Hebrides during the hard times of the previous century to a new life in America, the third, just published book, ending in present-day America and the Hebrides where his saga had originated.

Kyle's wince came and went in a flash.

'I didn't mean. . .' She began to backtrack and dropped her eyes to the book, staring at the cover as if she had never seen it before.

'What do you find so fascinating about the cover?' Kyle sounded curious, in spite of himself.

Briony lifted her eyes from the book. 'Her dress — the woman's on the cover — it — '

'Her dress?' Kyle cut in, baffled — until he laughed. 'Yes, of course. To each his own — her own, rather.' The combination of comment and irritated laugh instantly dismissed her reply as yet another predictable example of her one-track mind, which, Kyle was implying, couldn't think past clothes even when it came to covers of books.

Briony resented that but was relieved he'd cut her off before she had completed what she was going to say — that the woman's dress, turquoise and silky-looking, reminded her of one of her own which Kyle had loved. 'What I was going to say was that you've dressed Helena, and the other female characters, very. . .elegantly,' she improvised hurriedly.

'Thank you.' Kyle took it as a compliment when Briony was not at all sure she had meant it as one. 'As you know, I like elegant women. There's something about the image projected by a beautifully dressed, very sophisticated woman that I've always found very sexy. It makes a man want to touch, mould his hands over her, and then peel away the good-taste silks or cashmeres, or whatever, to reach the sensuous woman underneath them.'

The silky voice had the effect of teasing across her skin. Briony could feel his hands on her, his eyes undressing her without leaving her face, and, aware of the rise and fall of her breasts in the quickened breathing, she held his eyes fixedly to keep his from straying down to the tell-tale signs he had evoked by forcing those intimate images into her mind. . .of soft cashmere and silk being peeled off her body.

'Do you think I've managed to get that across with Helena, and my other women—the sensuality underneath the cool elegance?' Kyle's abrupt switch to the matter-of-fact tone might have had him putting the same question to a student in one of the literary workshops he sometimes conducted at the island school.

Briony ran the tip of her tongue over her suddenly dry lips and nodded jerkily. 'Yes, I suppose so,' she murmured on cue.

'And you were able to pick all that up just from the reviews?' Kyle's brow arched quizzically as he sprang her in her lie. 'How interesting.'

'I. . . I did glance through the book—last night

when I couldn't sleep.' She substituted her lie with another, even lamer one.

'As a change from counting sheep, was it?' He reached his hand out for the book as she was about to put it back on the table.

She went over to the desk and handed it to him. 'Actually, I think you've dressed them all a bit too elegantly,' she muttered, momentarily irrationally jealous of the fictional women that Kyle had dressed — and undressed — so expertly. With dozens of navy sweaters to vouch for his uninterest in his own clothes, Briony had always found it intriguing that he should have such an eye for what women wore — what she wore. Or was that *had worn*. . .?

'Do you think so?' Eyes up from the cover and lips pursed, he was looking her over slowly, as if making a mental inventory of her olive linen skirt, the creamy silk shirt and soft leather darker olive belt encircling her waist. Kyle's eyes meandered back up to her face. 'Isn't that curious when I dress them like you. . .?'

Elegant; sensuous; sexy. . . Was that how Kyle had seen her? Briony thought she had recognised something of herself in Helena, his heroine, but told herself it was only because she had wanted to see herself — wanted Kyle to have seen her that way. Now that he was confirming that he had used her as his model, the compliment hurt. His book had been written when they'd been happy together and he had loved her. . .loved the way she dressed, and everything about her. Not any more.

'Since I wasn't around last century when your saga began, I'm not sure how I'm supposed to take that.'

She rejected the compliment almost churlishly, by making out that she had missed the point. 'And anyway, you can't have used me for your model in the earlier books because you didn't know me then,' she pointed out with an edgy laugh.

'Then I must have conjured you up,' Kyle said unsmilingly.

While she couldn't understand what he meant, the odd change in his voice shot a shiver through her. They had veered into dangerous personal territory, with Kyle's slight of words unlocking too many images and memories that her nerves were in no state to cope with. 'Well, I won't keep you from your work any longer,' she said briskly to cover up her sudden tension. 'I only came in to tell you that my car is arriving this evening and——'

'Yes, I know, you've mentioned it before, and I'll be quite happy to drive you in to pick it up,' Kyle offered, all at once as remotely polite as if those unnerving double-meaning exchanges had not taken place.

'Oh, no, that's not what I came in for—thanks, anyway—I'm going to Castlebay now and Jimmy will be here any minute with the cab. I've got some things to do in the town,' she explained in response to Kyle's surprised glance at his watch. 'And there's someone I want to see,' she added, and knew she had said something wrong the moment Kyle's eyes iced over in a distancing stare.

'Do you indeed?' he queried coldly.

Eyes already lowered, he was reaching for his papers from the side of the desk in an unsubtle, officious dismissal that made her feel like a schoolgirl being sent from a very displeased headmaster's office, which instantly did away with her urge to protest that the someone was only Sara, an old lady she wanted to see about Hebridean knitting patterns, and not Martin Gunn. Briony stared down at the top of the black head for an angry moment, then spun on her heel and stormed from the room to wait outside the house for the cab.

How dared Kyle? How dared he? It wasn't his jumping to his conclusion, unwarranted as it was, that made her so furious, but that he was acting as if he had a right to that icy anger, when he himself was carrying on with Ishabel Macleod. Or didn't he realise that she knew — or at least guessed — what was going on between them?

Jimmy's usual one-sided commentary on Barra and the Universe left her free to stay silent and seethe in between the odd intermittent murmur of encouragement, and then, as her fury burnt itself out, Briony switched her mind to trying to figure out what Kyle could have meant by his 'conjuring up' comment. Visualising someone like her, the way people did their 'ideal' partner, she supposed, and for her it probably would have been a Kyle type of man if she'd ever taken the time to conjure anyone. Tall, dark, handsome, and intelligent with it, he matched most women's clichéd fantasy of their 'ideal', although Briony was quite certain that no woman could ever have visualised what the total Kyle Buchanan was all about, with his darkly exciting intensity that she had found so threateningly attractive in those first moments of their meeting; the passion in him which she had only sensed, and then very soon experienced, and responded to with her own, and not just in their physical relationship.

She had also responded to Kyle's passion for his island. . .his work. Her work too, which, until his about-turn in March, he had encouraged. . .been proud of, enjoying her successes as she had his. Yet, for all that, Briony found it hard to believe that Kyle could have had someone like her in mind before he met her, especially when he had been brought up with the fabulous-looking women of the Hebrides — like Ishabel Macleod. His heroines, too, were invariably dark, spirited, and with a Celtic background, if not actually Celtic. Except for Helena, his last heroine, a beautiful, sophisticated New York blonde coming back to find her roots in the Hebrides. And who had looked and dressed like the author's own wife.

'Sorry, Jimmy, what did you say?' Briony turned to him with an apologetic smile. He had asked a question while she had been staring into space, or, as she now realised, at the Street of Castlebay where Jimmy had already pulled up.

'I was asking if we'll be seeing you at the ceilidh tomorrow evening. Morag's granddaughter Hella will be performing on the clarsach and I'm sure you'll not be wanting to miss that.'

'I'm not quite sure. Possibly.' Briony equivocated, reluctant to tell him that she would be gone from the island before the concert — and every other event which she had so loved the previous year during that magical time when everything had been so wonderful between Kyle and herself and she had felt she belonged on this island.

She didn't feel that any more in spite of the smiles and 'lovely to see you again's that she had received on Monday, and was receiving now as she walked down the Street. Briony returned the greetings without being able to put names to half of the familiar faces. In the beginning, and particularly after the anonymity of London, it had disconcerted her that everybody appeared to know her—or, rather, know who she was: Kyle Buchanan's wife, or, perhaps, 'strange wife' who did something in London and came and went as the fancy took her. And when Kyle divorced her at the earliest legal opportunity they would probably only wonder that the marriage had lasted as long as it had—and hope he would soon settle down with a suitable local woman as he should have done in the first place. . .?

She had hours to fill but calling on Sara without notice at four-thirty was too close to the old lady's teatime, Briony decided, and changed her agenda to a visit to the castle instead, open to the public during the summer and a must for the tourists. Five of them were already boarding the little motor boat as she reached the small ramp beside the Street, and then— since one of them was Martin—if he hadn't seen her in the same moment she would have spun around and headed straight back where she came from.

'Hello, Briony; this is a pleasant surprise.' He was making room for her on the bench beside him. 'I was hoping we'd bump into each other,' he went on as she settled reluctantly into the boat. 'I did try to reach you at——'

'Goodness, haven't you made your grand tour of the castle yet? Shame on you,' she cut him off with a jarringly bright laugh before the mention of Reef House and Kyle came out.

'Yes, I have,' Martin returned after the slightly startled pause at her burst of gaiety. 'But I was at a bit of a loose end so thought I'd give the old place another going over. Is this your first visit?'

'No, I've seen it before too.' With Kyle as guide, naturally, and one who probably knew as much about it as its current, 46th Chief.

The run took only a few minutes and, once out of the confined space of the boat and in the restored courtyard of the castle, Briony relaxed again.

'I was going to say that I tried to telephone you yesterday.' Martin picked up where she'd cut him off. 'Did Buchanan pass on the message? He sounded none too pleased but did offer to bring you to the phone. It must be quite a way to the cottage; it was ages before he came back and said you weren't in.'

'Yes, he did mention you'd phoned. I was out at the time,' Briony said non-comittally, when she should have used the opportunity to tell him that Kyle would be more than just none too pleased if he telephoned again — unlikely, if she told him now who she was. As she should have done, except that now she felt dreadfully embarrassed at not having told him in the first place, and, after Kyle's reaction to the phone call, felt guilty just to be with him. . . nervous that Kyle might find out, which was ridiculous, because even if he did, what could Kyle do anyway? Hardly hurl her down into the dungeon below them that she and Martin were crossing by means of a walkway over the ghastly deep well-like thing into which victims had been hurled in more bloodthirsty centuries.

'Speaking of banquets,' Martin said suddenly as they trailed after a group into the banquet hall shortly afterwards, 'the reason I telephoned was to ask if you'd join me for dinner tonight — and perhaps come to the ceilidh with me tomorrow evening,' he added hopefully, even as she was shaking her head.

'I'm sorry, Martin, but I'm afraid it has to be no on both counts. I'm leaving Barra in the morning so I need to pack and have an early night tonight. I've just been waiting for my car to come in on the ferry this evening so I can sail with it tomorrow,' Briony explained with a smile, glad to have a genuine excuse for refusing instead of having to manufacture one.

Martin looked more surprised than disappointed. 'I take it you don't know, then? The ferry isn't due until nine tonight and won't be sailing tomorrow. Apparently it's developed some engine trouble — only minor, but they'll need to fly in some part or other from the mainland before they can fix it, and so I gather the sailing has been rescheduled for Saturday.'

'Saturday. . .?'

'That's right.' Martin grinned cheerfully. 'So why don't we have an early dinner now while we wait for it to come in and discuss tomorrow and the ceilidh over our meal?'

'Lovely,' murmured Briony mechanically, too distracted by the unexpected prospect of two more nerve-shredding days with Kyle to realise what she was saying, and trapped herself into an evening of Martin's non-stop light chatter when she was already feeling the strain of too much of his company for one day.

It wasn't Martin's fault; she would have felt the same in anybody else's company too. . .preoccupied, on edge, her mind on Kyle and how he would take the news of her extended stay. Aware that she was not exactly scintillating company herself, Briony was doing her best to pay attention to one of his anecdotes towards the end of the meal, when, to her surprise Martin's own attention switched from her very abruptly. She followed his eyes to the door, and tensed.

'Hello, there, Ishabel,' Martin called out in a too loud, too bright voice and with his face a searing red.

Ishabel glanced across at them and nodded at Martin without smiling, and then, it seemed to Briony, the sooty blue-black eyes looked right through her before Ishabel turned away to drift across the room with no acknowledgement of the small nod Briony had felt obliged to give out of ingrained politeness.

'That was Ishabel Macleod,' Martin said superfluously.

'Yes,' said Briony, seizing up, not so much at seeing Ishabel, but at the way the girl had so deliberately ignored her — snubbed her, Briony realised, piqued, and took it as a pointed confirmation that Ishabel now knew that Ms Hayward was Mrs Kyle Buchanan, presumably because Kyle had spoken to her since the airport meeting. 'Do you know her well?' she put to Martin suddenly.

'Yes. Well, no, not really — but not for want of trying.' Martin confessed ruefully. 'She's originally from Harris but has been on Barra since the end of last year when her family came here to take over this pub. I. . .' He hesitated, then blurted, 'I was awfully keen on her and. . .well, I thought I stood a chance — until I realised she was interested in someone else.' The bitterness jarred through the attempted laugh. 'The guy you're renting your cottage from actually — Kyle Buchanan. He's the one she always seems to be with whenever I've come in here.'

No islander would have told her that to her face, nor Martin either if he'd had an inkling that he was talking to Kyle Buchanan's wife, but, since he had not told her anything more than she had sensed — suspected from the moment she saw Ishabel with Kyle at the airport, Briony couldn't understand why she felt so shocked at hearing it said aloud; as if it were news to her that there was another woman in Kyle's life. The odd, breathless sensation of being stunned lasted only a moment and then she felt all right again, very calm, and curiously emotionless. As if something inside her had died. Her last lingering hopes of a reconciliation, she supposed.

CHAPTER FIVE

SHE knew Kyle was somewhere behind her because Morag's eyes swerved suddenly from her face to past her left shoulder. Briony tensed but didn't turn around. 'So if you would tell Sara that I'd like to drop in this afternoon, I'd appreciate it. I'd prefer she knew I was coming but I can't ring her because she's not on the telephone.' She recapped what they'd been talking about since Morag had come into the drawing-room and found her waiting for Kyle to finish on the extension phone in his study so that she could ring the pier office to book herself on Saturday's sailing.

'She doesn't believe in new-fangled inventions.' Morag flashed a brief grin. 'Some old folk around these parts don't, you know. Aye, I'll pass on your message when I pop in on her after shopping, and I'd best leave now or Neil will drive off without me. Is there anything you want me to get you in town?'

Briony shook her head and finally turned around to see Kyle propping up the doorway on the other side of the room.

'Nothing I need either, thank you, Morag.' Kyle moved aside to let the housekeeper pass into the hall. 'Good morning, Briony.' Hands in pockets, he wandered into the room, looking as he always looked in his moody navys — darkly handsome — and sounding perfectly normal.

Briony wondered at herself for being surprised. How had she expected him to look, sound, this morning? Guilty because she now knew for certain about him and Ishabel. . .? But Kyle didn't know that she knew and, even if he had known, would it have made any difference to him? Would he have started offering overdue explanations, regrets. . .? Briony doubted it.

'Hello, Kyle. I'm not on the ferry, as you see. It has engine trouble and won't be sailing until Saturday so I can't leave for another two days,' she told him with a forced casualness, and unnecessarily, since he would have learnt that already from Morag at breakfast. Briony would have told him herself when she returned from Castlebay the previous night if he hadn't been in his room with the door closed. 'I've just been waiting for you to finish on the phone so I can call the pier about Saturday's sailing.'

'Yes, I thought that's what you might have intended doing, so I undertook to telephone for you,' Kyle informed her helpfully, as if he had done her a favour.

Was he so anxious that she catch the first boat out that he couldn't even leave it to her to make the booking. . .? It certainly looked like it, and in spite of everything it hurt.

'Thank you,' she rallied, ultra-politely, and watched him wander over to the fireplace midway between the door and where she was by the piano in the far corner by the window which gave on to the sea.

Kyle smiled wryly. 'You might consider the thanks premature when I tell you that you're out of luck and

Saturday's sailing is completely booked out. Nuisance for you,' he put in regretfully, 'but I'm afraid even my influence couldn't stretch to getting you a place.'

Briony couldn't check the brittle little laugh of bitter amusement at how blatantly Kyle was telling her he wanted her off the island. 'Well, thank you for trying. I know that if you could have managed it you would have. When does the next ferry come in? Monday night?' she asked briskly, hoping to sound as anxious to leave as he was to see her go.

Kyle nodded.

'So you've booked me on Tuesday's sailing?'

'Actually, no, since I didn't think you'd much fancy travelling with the sheep. Tuesday's ferry won't be taking passengers, but sailing to South Uist to load up with sheep for the mainland,' he clarified in response to her frown of incomprehension. 'However, if you really want to be on it, I dare say I could try to speak to someone about it.'

Briony ignored the facetious offer. 'Then Wednesday's ferry sailing Thursday is the earliest I can leave?' she asked, slowly, after her mental run through the ferry schedule. 'Today week. . .?'

'That's right, today week,' Kyle confirmed carelessly, leaving his place by the fireplace and strolling over to her by the piano.

He had drawn up too close and was watching her too intently while she tried to come to terms with having to spend another seven days with a man who didn't want her around when only a few moments ago the prospect of another two days had seemed unbearable. Briony took a nervous little step away from him and bumped into the piano stool behind her.

'There's no need to vault piano stools in alarm, Briony.' Kyle flashed his teeth in a mirthless smile. 'I've no intention of using your extended stay under the conjugal roof, as I believe the term is, to start making advances, if that's what's making you so nervous about another week in my company. I thought I had already made it clear that I've made all the moves I intend to make. And you must agree I've made more than my share of them in all the flying up and down the country like a demented homing pigeon because my wife preferred her exciting life in London to the prospect of dreary domesticity on a remote island.'

Briony stared at him blankly, then a little wildly as her mind finally made the leap from delayed sailings to the breakdown of their marriage, and Kyle's crazy distortion of her need to be based in London.

'That is not fair,' she reacted at last, angrily. 'And not — ' The 'true' was lost in the unpleasant laughing sound which was not a laugh.

'Wrong tense, Briony. *Was* not fair,' Kyle corrected in the icy clipped tone that she hated. 'And not only not fair, but utterly incredible that I submitted myself to it. Still, I suppose it's a small consolation that you've finally caught on to just how unfair it was.' He twisted her words inside out and tossed them back at her with a twist of a satisfied smile at her shock and confusion.

'But I didn't. . . I mean, I wasn't — ' Briony broke off, completely at a loss as to what she should be denying or trying to explain. That she'd realised how unfair she had been to Kyle, or that she hadn't been unfair in the first place? 'I'm sorry if I caused you inconvenience,' she changed tack and retaliated with a sort of huffy dignity. 'Or ever gave you the impression that I was prepared to settle on Barra and make do with a spot of dressmaking on the side. I happen to be a designer,' she continued. 'And, incredible as it may seem to you, that makes me just as creative a person as you with your writing.'

Kyle was looking at her as if he didn't know what she was talking about, or didn't believe her, which made her even more furious. 'And if I wanted to set myself up so I could continue being a designer, it was no more than my right. And if you wanted me trapped in "dreary domesticity" surrounded by ump-teen children, then it's a pity you didn't think of reviving that ancient clan custom you once told me about. What was it called — handfasting. . .? One year and one day for the liaison to result in a baby, otherwise it was go your separate ways, that was it, wasn't it? And so much less trouble than marriage and divorce. Perhaps you should have tried it instead of marrying me.' Her voice shook dreadfully with the anger too long locked inside her, and she was as shocked as Kyle by its explosive release.

The colour had swept from his face leaving it very white against the blackness of his hair and furious dark eyes, and she thought that, for once, he was going to lash right back at her in his own anger — and was mistaken.

Kyle laughed. 'Your recollection of ancient Celtic social customs is very gratifying, but isn't it rather off beam?' he struck back at her with the familiar hateful sarcasm instead. 'Because if you're accusing me of having wanted to keep you barefoot and pregnant while you hunched over a hot sewing machine, then just how do you reconcile my two and a half years in London encouraging you in your damned career — let alone the six months of flying back and forth after we made the move here?'

Then why not another three months? she might have hurled at him, only there was no need to now since she had already found out why not. Briony shook her head in mute frustration.

'No, it doesn't fit in, does it? So don't go putting words into my mouth, even in retrospect, because I won't stand for it,' Kyle warned in a sudden spurt of harshness before turning angrily away from her. Halfway across the room he swung to her again. 'And next time you plan to give dinner a miss try to show a little consideration towards Morag and tell her, so she's not put to the trouble of preparing it for you if you're not going to be here to eat it.'

Briony flushed at the high-handed, adult-to-child reprimand. 'If you're talking about last night then I've already apologised for the oversight and have been told by Morag that I did not cause her undue inconvenience, let alone the mountain of trouble you're implying I caused by dining in Castlebay.'

'With Martin Gunn.'

It wasn't a question but her first instinct was to deny it. 'We did have a meal together while we waited for the ferry, yes,' she admitted because it would have been pointless not to when she had been seen by dozens of people and word could get back to Kyle by any number of them, Ishabel included. 'But only because we just happened to come across each other earlier, which isn't difficult to do in a place the size of Castlebay,' she justified herself heatedly, and resented that she felt the need to when she owed Kyle no explanation.

'That's your story and you're sticking to it?' Kyle smiled grimly. 'Just don't push your luck with any more fortuitous "comings across each other" during the next week, will you, Briony?'

Briony stared after the disappearing back in a mixture of helplessness and anger. He had not believed her and it should not have mattered any more what Kyle believed, thought or felt about her. Yet it did matter and his every accusation, every distortion hurt, while the bitterness underlying his anger had shocked her into distortions of her own, no less unfair than Kyle's. Briony had to admit, since there had never been the remotest question of Kyle expecting her to give up designing to turn housewife and mother before she was ready, and she certainly needed no reminding of how supportive he had been of her career——

Until Derek had sprung the extra three months on her and brought about the sudden change in Kyle's attitude. Had he really believed she'd been using her career as a pretext for not returning to Barra and decided enough was enough? Or simply used those extra three months as an excuse, to walk out of the marriage with a clear conscience, so to speak. . .? She would never be certain, but, either way, the result was the same: no more 'dreary domesticity' with Kyle—a cruelly belittling term for the day-to-day life they had shared and which she had loved, and wanted as much as Kyle. And still wanted, but which Ishabel would be sharing with him in her place, thought Briony bleakly, and was only thankful that she had not ended up hurling the name of Ishabel Macleod at him in jealous rage. That would have been more than her already bruised pride could have borne.

A ceilidh, even during the Feis, was not a dressing-up occasion; people came in everyday clothes, so the black silk jersey dress was rather overdoing it. It was one of several dressier outfits brought along for the odd dinner Briony had anticipated she would be invited to — and had been, by managers of some of the mills she had visited. Knee-length, with long sleeves and a high neck, the ubiquitous little black dress would have been almost puritanical but for the luxuriousness of the soft material, and the sensuous-ness that was all but sexiness of the figure-skimming line. The flat black shoes and hair worn down and caught back into a tail low on the nape combined to avoid the too clichéd elegance of hair piled up and high heels, but didn't take away from the distinct aura of sophistication that she projected. And meant to project. Because Kyle liked elegant, sophisticated women. . . Maybe he did, but it hadn't stopped him leaving her, Briony reminded herself bitterly when her consciousness caught up with the direction her subconscious had taken in what she realised was an attempt to draw Kyle's attention back to the kind of woman he had fallen in love with.

But to what purpose when he was no longer in love with her. . .? When he was barely speaking to her, as she had found out later in the morning when she had sought him out in his study to tell him she'd like to go to the ceilidh — a peace-making gesture after their horrible exchange. All Kyle had said was that he would be leaving at eight if she wanted to go with him, and had sounded as if he did not care one way or the other.

Now she had not seen him since their early dinner almost an hour ago — their first shared meal of her stay and with Morag already having left to attend the ceilidh with her family the strain had been awful. Kyle had been cold, distantly polite, while she had been tense and nervous, and reduced to making trite little observations about the weather when the silence became too much for her.

Before that, her afternoon had been spent in a visit to Sara about the knitting patterns, and then sitting upstairs in her room — doodling, as opposed to sketching, and wondering where Kyle was. He had been away from the house when she was in it, returning only just before dinner, and what he had been doing in his pointed effort to avoid her Briony had no idea and didn't ask.

'Ready?'

She swung her head to the door, startled, and instantly rigid that Kyle had come into the bedroom without knocking, catching her off guard all the more after his deadly polite stand-off of the day.

He was already dressed, and, out of his island 'uniform' of dark jersey over dark trousers, he looked the Kyle of their London days in the dark suit and with the hard-edged sophistication about him: the Kyle of their first meeting when she hadn't been able to take her eyes off him. She dragged her eyes away from him now, aware that her heart had given the familiar out-of-rhythm little skip.

'Nearly,' she murmured, returning her eyes to the mirror on the dressing-table. She was sitting on the stool in front of it and had just finished putting on her make-up, which, like the dress, was an excessive gesture on an island where few women—other than tourists—wore any make-up. About to clip on the first of the chunky silver earrings, her hands paused at her ear while her eyes followed Kyle's reflection in the mirror as he strolled past her and seated himself on the foot of the bed behind her to wait for her to finish getting ready. It was something he had done countless times during their married life, and something he had seemed to like doing, but, while the trite routine was no doubt part of zillions of other couples' lives, it was not part of their life any more. Briony hurriedly clipped the earring on.

'You look very lovely.' Kyle met her eyes in the mirror without adding even a perfunctory smile to go with the compliment.

'Thank you.' She tried for nonchalance, and gave a small smile as a sort of reinforcement of how unperturbed she was by this impromptu replay of one of their domestic scenes, until the next moment she gave her nervousness away in the jerky reach for the second earring which sent the heavy piece of silver off the dressing-table and on to the floor. 'Butter fingers,' she reprimanded herself with a breathless little laugh, and leaned down to pick it up from beside the stool, only Kyle reached it before she did. He scooped it up and held it out to her when she straightened.

Briony tossed back the tail of hair which had swung to the front of her shoulder in her reach to the floor, then took the earring from him. 'Thank you,' she murmured, and went to lift it to her ear.

'Just a moment; you haven't pulled the zip right up to the top.' Kyle returned her hair to the front again and stepped behind her to do up the zip for her, as any other husband might have done.

Hands on her lap, Briony was hardly breathing as his fingers sought the concealed tag under the fold of material, her own fingers crushing around the earring in her left hand and digging the hard silver into her palm. The mirror cut off Kyle's reflection at the shoulders so that she couldn't see his face, which somehow made it all the more unnerving just to sit there and feel the pressure of his fingers through the silky material, and knowing he could see her face and read whatever it was she was afraid was there to be read.

'Thank you,' she murmured yet again as the zip swished up the couple of inches to the neckline.

Kyle didn't say anything, not even a suavely careless 'Not at all'. His hand stayed at the back of her neck, resting there in light contact, and, very conscious of her own slowed-down breathing, she didn't move.

Then, as the silence extended itself, the tension between them extended itself with it, and into every niche and corner of the large room, it seemed to Briony while she waited—for Kyle's next move or her own. . .?

One of them was going to have to do something, say something, to break the mounting tension that was unmistakably sexual now, and heightening unbearably until Kyle placed his other hand on her shoulder and his face came into the mirror's range as he leaned over her. Their eyes locked for what seemed an age before Kyle went on to lower his head to her shoulder and then she gave a tremoring sigh, of relief more than satisfaction, as his lips finally touched the bare skin at the side of her neck in a long, very deliberate kiss.

She made the next move, a provocative arch of the neck to his lips, a blatant invitation Kyle took up. Slowly, sensuously, he moved his mouth up along the curve of her neck, and then slowly all the way back down. Briony closed her eyes as the familiar sensations ricocheted through her and had no awareness of reaching a hand into his hair until Kyle lifted it away, together with his mouth from her neck. She snapped her eyes open in surprise and saw that he had already straightened and his head and face were out of range again.

Lips slightly parted, cheeks flushed, her own face stared back at her from the mirror, looking exposed and vulnerable — a little absurd too, with one large chunky earring on; the other, forgotten, was still in her hand. In a sudden, agitated movement, she wrenched the one off her ear, and placed both of them on the dressing-table, and that confused, angry moment when she couldn't distinguish who had been seducing who was when she should have jumped to her feet and taken herself out of the room. Instead, she let Kyle draw her to her feet and into his arms, and, if there was a rational thought still lingering in her mind, it went completely by the board as she wound her arms around his neck and drew his face down to her hungrily.

This time Kyle was not playing any tantalising little games. Instantly, fiercely demanding, his tongue thrust deeply into her mouth while the hand at her back kneaded rather than stroked, and Kyle's fingers dug through the soft material of the dress as if he wanted to hurt her. The long swishing sound she associated with the zip only when Kyle pulled away from her to get the dress off her shoulders and arms in a hard, impatient tug, and, an instant later, plunged one hand into the lacy slip to close it over her breast.

Briony gasped with the shock of the touch and the sheer force of arousal that rocked through her. Agitatedly, she reached up and dragged the slip down herself to release her breasts for him. . .for hands, his searing gaze, and finally his mouth as she cradled his head to her on the wave of trembling, breathtaking pleasure from the caresses of Kyle's mouth and tongue at each nipple in turn, until the pleasure became too much, and, at the same time, too unsatisfying. Almost frantically, she drew his head away and up, from her breasts, and in a shaky scramble of fingers began to unbutton his shirt, sliding her hands in through the first gap in her need to touch him as he had touched her.

Kyle finished off the rest of the buttons himself, throwing off his jacket and wrenching himself out of the shirt and tie in his own barely restrained excitement, and when he crushed her in his arms again his aroused body felt hard and bruising, and wonderful against her softness.

Their mouths locked, Briony clung to him as he eased her towards the bed, and in the end it was she who broke off the intoxicating kiss, dragging her mouth away from his to tell him that she loved him. The words nearly blurted themselves out—would have blurted themselves out, if it hadn't been for her shock when she looked into Kyle's eyes.

'I want you,' Kyle said harshly, and everything about him told her that. . .his body, the desire—raw hunger—glittering at her from the dark depths of his eyes, and with nothing else in them but that.

Their bodies seemed to be in a frenzy for each other, and yes, in spite of himself maybe, Kyle wanted her as much as she wanted him. Wanted her body and was more than willing to take it if it was on offer—then tell her later that it had been 'for old times' sake'? How could she be sure that he wouldn't? She couldn't, any more than she could be sure that their lovemaking would blot out Ishabel Macleod forever from Kyle's mind.

Narrowed to darkly lashed slits, Kyle's eyes bored into her face where every emotion, her every doubt, must have been laid bare for him in that long moment when the last of the honeyed warmth of her arousal ebbed away. Briony unwound her arms from around his neck. She was shaking her head long before she realised she was doing it.

'No, Kyle. No. . .' she whispered despairingly. Not this way, in blind, overwhelming passion. Not until I know that you love me again, she wanted to cry out, and tried to pull away from him before her own body colluded with his in seducing her into abandoning all reason and self-respect for the dangerous pleasure of a night in Kyle's arms, perhaps for the very last time.

Kyle tightened his hold, his hands ruthlessly hard at the small of her back as he locked their bodies against — into — each other again until she gasped at the sudden renewed warmth flaring deep inside her. Kyle's lips curved in angry satisfaction at her betrayal of her involuntary physical response to him. 'Don't ever lead me on again, Briony.' Keeping one hand in place at her back, he brought the other around to cup her jaw without any gentleness as he lifted her face and held it immobile. His own face was so close that Briony could feel his breath on her mouth and thought he was going to kiss her again, and if he did she knew she would be lost. 'Don't start anything unless you mean to see it through, *mo gràdh*,' he warned, the softness menacing, the *'mo gràdh'* — 'my love' — a mockery. Then he released her so abruptly that she nearly fell.

The end of the bed was behind her. Lowering herself to it, she watched dazedly as Kyle snatched up his shirt and jacket off the floor.

'I'll be waiting downstairs,' he told her in a sudden switch to cold anger, and walked out without another glance at her.

Had she started it? Led Kyle on? If she had it had been by not leaping to her feet but staying put when he had walked into the room, a move some part of her mind had interpreted as a sexual overture despite Kyle's acid assurance only that morning that he had no intention of initiating anything sexual between them. But, whichever of them had sent out the first signal, every little move after that had led inexorably to the next. . .to her own and Kyle's passion, which for short, ecstatic moments she had deluded herself came with love, realising almost too late that for Kyle it was only desire. . .physical need. Sex. A chance to win Kyle back, maybe, but a chance she could not risk taking, knowing as she did that great sex didn't automatically make for a great marriage. If it did, then theirs would have been the marriage of the century, and it was bitter irony that the physical attraction that had bonded them together in a conservatory in Holland Park three and a half years ago should still be so vibrantly strong between them when nothing else was. But she wanted more from Kyle than sex, and if he couldn't — wouldn't — give her his love then she would only end up hating herself for succumbing to her need of him, and perhaps hating Kyle for playing on that need.

Briony hauled herself back into the dress, hauled up the zip to its last millimetre and put on the earrings. Only pride made her go downstairs and face Kyle when she would have given anything to stay in her room and never emerge again.

He was by the front door as she came down the stairs into the hall, and had the air of someone who'd just stopped pacing. His tension radiated at her from yards away, as hers must have at him. He threw her a quick glance, almost of concern, when she reached him — to check that she hadn't been crying and looked too awful to be seen in public with him. . .? Briony turned her face from him and they went out of the house in silence, and drove the four-odd miles in the same thick silence like any other couple who'd just had a monumental row and had to go out together straight after it. To put on a public front, in their case at a concert which might as well have been a funeral, thought Briony miserably as Kyle drove them slowly past the parked cars and groups of people outside the school building just beyond the town. Its modern facilities provided the venue for a lot of the island's community activities, like tonight's ceilidh, which had drawn an appreciable gathering, and Kyle had to drive well past the school to park.

She stumbled over some stones as they started the walk back up the sloping road. Instantly, Kyle put out a hand to steady her, and then took her hand and put it through his arm. The physical contact was unbearable after what had just transpired between them in the bedroom, but Briony didn't protest or try to draw away from him because they were already the focus of dozens of curious eyes watching their approach.

CHAPTER SIX

BRIONY was used to curious eyes. Barra or London, New York even, they made a striking couple. Kyle with his dark good looks, and she with her blonde, but here on Barra there was much more to it than the casual interest of a passer-by. Mrs Kyle Buchanan was back after nearly a year. Was the marriage over or wasn't it? She could read the question in their eyes, behind the smiles. . .in the polite greetings, and wondered whether she was being paranoid, or whether Kyle also felt the curiosity that was fairly pulsating around them.

Henrik Bergen must have been on the look-out for them, materialising out of the crush as they entered the foyer. 'Good evening Kyle. And Miss Hayward, what an unexpected pleasure to see you again,' he greeted her with a beam.

'A pleasure to see you too, Professor Bergen.' Briony managed a smile, disconcerted somewhat by the 'Miss Hayward' after the chorus of 'Mrs Buchanan's directed at her, which the professor had apparently missed, or not taken in. Did he still not know that she was Kyle's wife, or was he punctiliously sticking to the Miss Hayward because that was how Kyle had introduced her?

'I did not realise you would be coming with Kyle this evening.' He turned the beam of pleasure on Kyle.

'Glad you could make it, Henrik,' Kyle returned without any explanation of how she came to be with him, and was disengaging his arm from under her hand as he spoke. 'I'd better see about the tickets.'

'I have mine already, thank you.' The professor brandished the ticket in his hand as evidence.

'Right, then I'll just get ours. Excuse me, will you, Briony, Henrik?' He left them to make his way towards the front desk set up outside the entrance into the hall while Briony distractedly tried to give her attention to the professor as he launched into what threatened to be a long account of his trip to the tiny abandoned island of Mingulay the previous day.

It was a very long account, lasting until Kyle's return, with Martin Gunn, astonishingly, at his side, and then, the next moment, embarrassingly, at her side.

'So you managed to come after all! That's great.' Martin grinned delightedly.

'Hello, Martin.' Briony jerked a smile and risked a glance at Kyle, who met her eyes in a cold, impenetrable stare.

Then nobody said anything. They all just stood there, Martin and the professor vaguely expectant, which was when she realised that Kyle and Martin had not become acquainted somewhere along the line but had simply happened to arrive at the same destination together, and if there were to be any introductions they were up to her. Briony made them, flusteredly, and, in the ensuing round of handshakes, was very conscious of Kyle's icy civility towards Martin. . .of Martin's nervousness and too much grinning; only the professor was cheerily unaware of the tension sparking around him.

'Excuse me again, will you?' Kyle said the moment the introductions were over, and, with a nod at no one in particular, turned and walked away from them.

With some of the people already gone into the hall, the foyer had thinned of its crowd, so when Briony turned to see where Kyle was going she saw Ishabel immediately. The girl was standing alone by the central pillar only a couple of yards away, close enough to have heard the conversation, and close enough to have joined the group if she had chosen to. She had chosen to wait for Kyle to join her instead. Briony watched the glowing smile light up her face, bringing the almost frigid beauty to life, but this time, unlike at the airport, Briony made herself look at Kyle's face too, watched it light up with returned warmth, and felt everything inside her tighten suddenly, painfully, at what she was seeing. It was only a confirmation of what she knew already — and accepted, she had told herself, and yet the sensation was as sharp and as fresh as it had been at the airport; at Morag's veiled hint; at Martin's innocent disclosure. It was instant shock, instant jealousy all over again. She had been lying to herself about accepting the liaison. She had not accepted it at all.

They were speaking in Gaelic; Briony could hear their voices but couldn't distinguish a word. Did she really want to? Wasn't it enough to see the transformation from the tense, grim Kyle who had been with her to the warmly smiling Kyle who was with Ishabel now, to see Ishabel leaning towards him as she spoke and Kyle bending his head to her, and both so absorbed in each other that they seemed unaware of anybody else in the foyer.

Their stunning dark looks alone would have attracted attention; the fact that it was Kyle Buchanan, local celebrity, with the local beauty guaranteed that every eye was on them. That was what was adding to the turmoil inside her — that Kyle was so deliberately, so blatantly pairing off with Ishabel. In public, and just yards away from his own wife. And after he had so nearly swept her into bed barely an hour ago. . . Briony couldn't believe it; didn't want to believe what her appalled eyes were seeing.

'I'm sorry, Professor. . .?' She turned an ashen face to him and tried to pull herself together as she met Henrik Bergen's kindly curious gaze.

'Mr Gunn has been suggesting I attempt the climb up the hill behind Brevig to inspect the ancient standing stone.' The professor's attempt to draw her into the conversation had her staring at him blankly.

'Are you interested in standing stones youself, Miss Hayward?'

Standing stones. . .? She would die of embarrassment if the hysterical laugh welling in her throat burst out. 'Oh, yes, avidly,' Briony assured him through a mad little cackle which, to her relief, she managed to stifle dead, but she couldn't manage to do anything about the compulsion that drew her eyes back to Kyle. Somewhere at the back of her dazed mind was an awareness that she must be attracting attention herself as she stood there like one of the professor's standing stones, transfixed by a sight that must have been commonplace around the island for months.

'We are to go in.' Professor Bergen took her elbow, and, short of breaking free and trying to run out of the building, Briony had no option but to allow him to lead her to Kyle — and Ishabel, who acknowledged them all with a slight nod then moved on ahead towards the hall, while Kyle gave them a quick glance and followed her, so that it looked as if he was with Ishabel and not the trio bringing up the rear.

Then, inexplicably, since Ishabel and Kyle had been ahead of them, it was Henrik who led the way into their row of seats, the fifth up from the front and just across from the doorway. Briony went in after him with Martin at her heels, and Ishabel would have been next except that while she and Kyle were still standing an incredibly ancient-looking couple came in and hovered beside them. Immediately, Kyle ushered them into his and Ishabel's seats, and then, after a swift scan of the hall, put a hand on Ishabel's arm and guided her down the aisle and into the second row and the two vacant seats in the middle of it.

Briony had a perfect view. Barely seated, Ishabel was already leaning to Kyle to murmur something, and after the lights went down she could still see the dark heads repeatedly drawing together for more murmured exchanges.

'See what I meant about Ishabel and Buchanan?' Martin murmured breathily into her own ear.

Briony could see nothing else from the concert's

start to finish. The items came and went in a barely registered blur. Morag's granddaughter at the clarsach—the Scottish harp, which she usually loved—could have been crashing cymbals, while the one-act little Gaelic play performed by the children was just so much sound which she applauded vigorously along with everybody else.

The beautiful unaccompanied Gaelic singing did break through her wall of misery, though, perversely only to make her more miserable. Invariably of unrequited love, the poignant melodies in the clear lilting voices had always made her want to weep, and, eyes glued on the black-haired couple three rows in front of her, Briony felt like weeping now, only she knew that if she started she might never stop. She was glad when the segment was over and tried to concentrate on the piper who came after it. Bagpipes always reminded her of old Shonny whiling away his solitary nights in his cottage, and the next thought led back to Kyle, and Ishabel, and she was back where she started from, although with an anger edging through her hurt. How dared Kyle show her up—humiliate her like this in front of the locals? How could he? It seemed too cruel to be true—that he had arranged to meet Ishabel at the ceilidh and yet had made those advances in the bedroom. Or allowed her to make them to him. Either way was equally, unbelievably cruel, and Briony's one tiny consolation was that she had not given in to her need of him.

It was over; the lights had come up. She rose mechanically after the final round of applause. The professor was voicing rapturous, if slightly pedantic

approval of the 'display of true Gaelic spirit' on the
one side of her while on the other Martin seemed to
be saying how pleased he was that she wouldn't be
leaving the island for another week. She must have
told him that herself, Briony supposed, but couldn't
remember. He was still talking as they left the hall
and might have been talking in Gaelic for the little
she managed to take in.

When Kyle came out into the foyer it was with
Morag and the local doctor at his side and Ishabel
nowhere in sight, Briony noted. Ignoring his
approach, she concentrated on Martin's wrap-up of
some feature or other of Vatersay, and realised,
startled, that he was saying he would be taking her
to see it after their picnic on Saturday. What picnic?
What on earth had she agreed to in those last
moments in the hall. . .? Whatever it was, she would
have to renege on it, but later. For the moment she
kept up the smiling and nodding, chatting even,
during the general goodbyes on the pavement. The
instant they parted from the rest and she and Kyle
were alone in the car, Briony went into a miserable
tight-lipped silence and couldn't believe it when Kyle
actually began to comment about the concert, pleasantly, casually, as if absolutely nothing untoward had
happened between them. . .no heavy scene in the
bedroom. . .no Ishabel waiting for him in the foyer.

On the other side of Castlebay he stopped the one-
sided commentary and switched to humming one of
the songs they had just heard. '*Thig Trì Nithean Gun
Iarraidh*': 'Three things come without asking', a song
based on an old Gaelic saying: 'Three things come
unasked: love, jealousy and fear'. Composed just for

her. . .? It was one of the songs that had most made her want to weep, and, while Kyle was probably only humming it because it had been the last song sung and he was familiar with it anyway, Briony felt that he was humming it deliberately to torment her. She stood it for about a mile and then couldn't stand it any longer.

'For God's sake, Kyle, stop it,' she lashed out at him suddenly, angrily, and almost in tears, and startled him into sweeping his eyes off the road to throw her an astonished look. 'Just stop it, please,' she mumbled, and swung her face away to stare out of the window at the brooding hill with the professor's standing stone out of eyes' range behind an old army shack.

Kyle stopped the humming and the silence was worse. Aware of his intermittent glances at her, Briony refused to look at him and had her hand on the door-handle as they came down the last stretch of drive, ready to leap out the moment the car stopped.

'Briony, wait.' Kyle caught her by the arm and turned her towards him. 'About this evening,' he said in a strained voice. 'I know you're upset, and I just want to say that I didn't mean it to happen the way it did.'

Briony stared at him in a combination of disbelief and a kind of shocked fascination, then gave a small angry laugh out of sheer helplessness, and couldn't begin to understand what was going on behind that hard, handsome face of the man she had thought she knew, loved—and still loved—and who, having hurt and humiliated her, was now blithely dismissing the grotesque evening as some little slip-up.

'I have a headache, Kyle, and would like to go straight to bed, if you don't mind.' It was the only thing she could think of to say.

Kyle wanted to say something more. She could see that, and also that he was annoyed—or was it puzzled?—that she was ignoring his 'apology'. That made her want to hit him and she was really afraid that she might—or, worse, break down and cry in front of him, if she didn't get away immediately. 'Let me go, Kyle, please,' she ordered agitatedly, and, the moment he released her, scrambled out of the car and ran into the house.

For the first time since her arrival on Barra, she slept right through the night. Her mind a self-protective blank, there was no futile hashing and rehashing of the day, the evening. . . Kyle; Ishabel. She simply fell asleep the moment her head touched the pillow and woke the next morning feeling. . .not refreshed. . .just blank, and lay listening to the birds and sheep, and splashing of water over the rocks. Curiously loud splashing, explained when she turned her head to the window and saw the dull grey sky instead of the clear sharp blue of the previous day.

Briony didn't mind. She loved the grey, the rain, even the howling winds that sometimes could make it a feat to keep a door open long enough to go out through it. It was the way her memory always conjured up the island when she was in London. The Barra of the first week with Kyle. . .the walks along a wild sea, watching the rain lash the windows as she sat by a peat fire with Kyle, talking—about every-

thing — and feeling safe and warm, and with the sense
of being complete. . .that everyone and everything
she wanted was on this small remote island. Her
home and the home of the children she and Kyle
would have. And had never had the chance to have.

Had she been wrong putting off starting the family
which might have welded her and Kyle more completely together, wrong to have wanted the fulfilment
of her work as well and devoting the time to setting
herself up so that she could continue to have her
career in the future? The career that had inadver-
tently taken her away from Kyle and the island for
too long and left him susceptible to another
woman — through loneliness, as Morag had
implied. . . The sort of loneliness she felt without
Kyle. And would feel the rest of her life when she
left Barra next week. In six days' time.

Six more days with Kyle. To endure. . . Briony
didn't know how she felt any more. Last night, hurt
and humiliated by the sight of Kyle and Ishabel
together, she would have clung grimly to the wing of
any plane to get herself off the island and away from
him. This morning, all her pain and anger — about
everything — seemed to have gone and she only felt
worn out, traumatised by the too numerous
emotional demands of the previous day. . .the horrible confrontation of the morning, the unleashed
passion in the bedroom, the final shock of Kyle's
public betrayal of her. Was it any wonder her mind
had withdrawn into a comforting cocoon of
blankness. . .?

The kitchen clock showed eleven when she went
downstairs. Morag was out, or in her own small flat

along the passage leading off the kitchen. Briony raided the fridge, made herself an enormous breakfast-cum-lunch, then ate it with an appetite that surprised her. Kyle had been in his study when she had gone past. In there to work, or to avoid her? she wondered as she went past the closed door again on her way to the box-room to ferret out a pair of her old wellies.

With Kyle's rainproof jacket over her sweater and jeans, and a sketchpad stuffed into the pocket, she let herself out of the back door and wandered down to the water's edge.

Pulling her hair free from its clasp, she just walked and walked, into the wind. . .against the wind. How long she walked, Briony had no idea. She had not bothered to put on her watch since time was irrelevant and she had no plans for what was left of the day but to do whatever she felt like doing. And she felt like walking with the wind in her hair. Later, she settled in the shelter of rocks up from the wave-beaten shore and sketched. . .the curve of coast with the gigantic monolithic rock of Muldoanich in the distance in the south; the blurry outline of the Cuillins of Skye across the water; the brooding face of Reef House. Clothes. The designs, once started, came in a tumble from her mind as if they couldn't wait to hit the page; swirls of hooded capes, jackets loose and boxy, jackets streamlined and straight. . . skirts, trousers, and dozens of softly flowing evening outfits for the cashmere in all its glorious colours, but mainly for the mauve-tinged blues and dusky pinks of heather over the treeless hills.

And she saw them all on a tall, beautiful dark

woman striding with arrogant grace along a picturesque tiny street which turned into a frenetic New
York avenue without a missed stride, or drifting
equally sensuously through a banquet hall of a castle
in the sea, or the foyer of the New York Met. It was
only when she stopped the almost frenzied flight of
pencil across paper that Briony realised the shape of
the faceless model was Ishabel Macleod, and somehow was not surprised. She had never drawn faces
into the shapes; now she went back over them and
put Ishabel's face into every sketch. Then she sat
there for ages and just stared at the sea.

The Hebridean Collection was Ishabel's collection.
Every design had, if subconsciously, sprung into
being with Ishabel in mind. . ... Ishabel in sweeping
stark black cashmere. Ishabel in white cashmere. . .
in the heather-touched cashmeres and tweeds. . .
Ishabel now intruding into her work as if it hadn't
been enough that she had intruded into her life with
Kyle.

Briony snapped closed the sketchpad, rammed it
into her pocket and began picking her way over the
stony path back up the slope to the house, and was
halfway up when she saw Kyle coming down towards
her. Instantly her tension was there, her hurt of the
previous night springing back as raw as if she were
seeing him in rapt tête-à-tête with Ishabel Macleod
again.

'What have you been doing? It's five o'clock and
you've been down here for hours. You'll catch your
death of cold, if you haven't already.' Kyle's voice
held a belligerent concern like Morag's when she
growled admonishment about not dressing warmly

enough, going out in the wind, and a host of other misdemeanours.

It was a show of concern that Briony didn't want from him. 'I'll try not to "end up an invalid on your hands".' She quoted his words from the night of the storm back at him and didn't miss Kyle's flash of scowl at her sarcasm as she passed him to walk on ahead. 'Yes, I know it's a mess,' she laughed irritably, catching the glance at her hair while she was attempting to smooth it down once near the house and out of the wind.

Kyle suddenly lifted a hand to it in a half-reach, as if he wanted to touch it or brush it away from her face, then thought better of it and dropped his hand to his side. He had always loved her hair. . .loved running his fingers through it, mesmerised almost by its honeyed blonde silkiness, and she had always loved his touch. The gesture — his momentary urge to touch it now — had been nothing more than habit, and Briony resented the ties to their past that he hadn't yet quite managed to shake off.

'Morag's laid out afternoon tea in my study. The fire's going; come in and get yourself warm,' Kyle ordered as she gave a shiver.

Briony hesitated. 'Yes, all right,' she agreed not very graciously, warily taking her cue that the previous night — entire day — had never happened, and, given the circumstances, acting like civil strangers was possibly the only way they would be able to see out her enforced stay in Reef House. 'Thank you,' she added on a polite afterthought, pulling off her gumboots and following him into the house through the door along from his study. 'Thank you,' she repeated politely when Kyle helped her out of his jacket and tossed it over the high-backed chair against the wall as he went past it.

Kyle's study was a beautiful room at any time; with the fire in the grate it projected the cosiness and mellowness that she remembered so well and which was so intrinsically part of the times she did not want to be reminded of any more.

'Scones, how lovely. I adore Morag's scones.' The sentiment was genuine; the trilly attack of nerve-induced enthusiasm made it ring false. Briony hurriedly began to pour out the tea, automatically, without being asked, while Kyle stood by the fire, arm resting on the mantelpiece, watching her in a replay of yet another of their domestic scenes. Briony met his eyes briefly as she handed him his cup, then took her own and went to the window from which Kyle must have watched her route-march on the shore, pacing. . .whatever out of her system. Had she. . .? Nowhere near it if her nervousness and tension were any indication, and, as if sensing this, Kyle started to talk about his writing, a safe neutral subject, and went on to tell her about a play he had commenced and which was set in London.

'London. . .?'

He smiled faintly at her surprise. 'I think I've written the Hebrides out of my system and want to try something completely different — expand my horizons and leave the Celts to Henrik for a while. Incidentally, I've invited him over for dinner tomorrow.'

Briony had left the window and come to sit, but not settle, in the armchair by the fireplace. Kyle had remained standing. She looked at him and said nothing.

Kyle's laugh sounded strained. 'We'll try not to bore you too much with tales of fairy mounds and ancient ruins, if that's what's bothering you.'

That was not what was bothering her, and it seemed incredible that he could not see what was; that, after what he had put her through last night, he could turn around and expect her to be in her 'place' as his wife, keeping up appearances in a domestic charade for his guest.

She would do it for the simple reason that, if she refused, Briony did not trust herself not to tell him why.

CHAPTER SEVEN

'YES, well, I'll try to be back in good time but I can't promise.' Briony put her cup down with a clatter and rose to her feet.

'Back from where?'

'From my earlier engagement.'

'What engagement?' The dangerous edge to his voice signalled that Kyle had added two and two very swiftly.

Briony had reached the door. 'With Martin Gunn. I've arranged to spend the day with him on Vatersay tomorrow,' she tossed at him with commendable offhandedness as she flung herself out of the room, and had made it to the first landing before Kyle caught up with her.

'Not so fast, Briony; we haven't finished our discussion yet. Or did you have in mind that we finish it in the bedroom?' Kyle's spuriously pleasant voice was more menacing than even the body barring her way up the stairs. 'No, I rather thought not.' He laughed shortly as she gave a quick shake of the head and backed away from him. 'However, I also thought I'd already suggested that you don't push your luck with any more encounters with Gunn. I might have bought one story of "coming across each other" but I certainly did not intend to buy any more and, as far as I'm concerned, last night at the ceilidh you pushed that luck far enough — not to mention my good manners and friendliness towards visitors to this island.'

Friendliness. . .? Briony yelped an involuntary laugh at Kyle's description of his chilling civility towards poor Martin.

Kyle smiled humourlessly. 'You find that amusing, do you? As amusing as introducing me to the man after I told you that I wouldn't tolerate you seeing him again?'

'I didn't ——'

'You're not in London now, Briony,' he snapped off her denial. 'And, whatever further arrangements you've made with him, you're going to have to cancel them, because I won't have my wife making a fool of herself on this island. Or of me.'

Briony had never heard such arrogant flaunting of the double standard in her life. One set of rules for her, no rules at all for Kyle. 'But it's all right for you, is it, to make one out of me?' she flung shakily at his back as he started down the stairs.

Kyle stopped and spun around, black brows peaking in the frown. 'What are you talking about?' he demanded in a quite creditable show of not having a clue.

It was touch and go, and part of her would have given anything to hurl the name of Ishabel Macleod into the open at last. Briony bit savagely into her lower lip to prevent the words she knew she would regret if she ever let them leave her mouth.

Kyle's frown cleared. 'Do go on, you have my full attention,' he drawled in mocking encouragement that told her he knew, or at least guessed, what she had been about to blurt out, and was daring her to go ahead.

Briony gave a mute shake of the head, turned and fled up the stairs and into her room. Slamming the door closed, she leaned back against it, not in expectation of Kyle following her in, but to steady herself. She was literally shaking, as well as shaken, at how close she had come to starring in one of those frightful, humiliating scenes in which the jealous wife railed about 'the other woman'; how very nearly Kyle had goaded her into trading in pride for a few short moments of retaliation.

What on earth were they doing to each other? Why were they doing it? How had a relationship which had commenced as the epitome of the cliché 'made for each other' degenerated into something so awful, with those two same people now wanting only to hurt each other? Not the two same people, but two strangers. Briony could no longer recognise herself in the inconsistent emotional woman see-sawing between the despair and anger left in the wake of Kyle's rejection of her. She could not recognise Kyle any more either. . .sarcastic, arrogant, and as bewilderingly inconsistent as herself when he paraded his liaison with Ishabel on the one hand and acted the Victorian husband on the other.

Of course she had no intention of seeing Martin tomorrow. Vaguely surprised that he had not tried to contact her about the picnic, she used the cover of a discussion with Morag about the next day's dinner to throw in a lame reason for needing Martin Gunn's telephone number and inveigled the unsuspecting old lady to track it down for her. Later, after she heard

Kyle leave the house, she rang Martin, and it was just as well that she had not intended to see him because Martin had no intention of seeing her.

Over a couple of drinks with Henrik Bergen after the ceilidh, he had apparently become acquainted — belatedly — with what most people on the island knew, and the professor among them it seemed: that Kyle Buchanan and Briony Hayward were husband and wife.

'You've made me feel rather an idiot, Briony,' Martin told her tersely, and all she could do was apologise and hang up, salving her conscience with the knowledge that he had not really been interested.

She had realised that after he had divulged his feelings about Ishabel. . .that it was simply distraction he was looking for. Or perhaps being seen with other women was by way of an attempt to get the beautiful girl to take notice of him. . .make Ishabel jealous. When she was so obviously absorbed in Kyle. . .? Poor Martin, if that was what he was trying to do, thought Briony with wry sympathy and was aware of the irony of being reduced to what amounted to the same pathetic exercise herself when she left the house at nine-thirty the next morning.

She slammed herself out loudly so that Kyle would hear her and assume that she was off to spend the day with Martin. And be jealous. . .? No, merely furious at her gesture of defiance, which, like her earlier stand about Shonny's cottage, came at a price, on this occasion in a long unenjoyed day of driving through intermittent rain up and down the island — the west side of it so as not to risk coming across Kyle on the east side.

Castlebay was off-limits for the same reason, and by mid-afternoon she was starving and would have thrown in the towel and returned to Reef House if the island's mobile grocer had not come past on his round as she sat in her car contemplating—yet again the tiny ruined tower of St Clair's Castle, all that remained of the castle that was not in the sea like Kisimul but in the waters of the large Loch St Clair under the shadow of Ben Tangaval towering ominously against the leaden sky.

After exchanging the mandatory comments on the change in the weather, he, like most locals she had come across to date, told her how nice it was to see her back, and she was surprised—and touched—at how genuinely pleased he seemed, adding to the irony that, of all the islanders, the only one not glad she was back was Kyle. And Ishabel. . .? Briony rather had the feeling that the return of Kyle's wife was an irrelevance as far as the girl was concerned.

She bought some biscuits and ate them watching the seals a couple of miles further along at Seal Bay, then continued the tourist beat to the Chille Bharra chapel on the northern end of the island where a glance through the door showed a troop of visitors wandering through the ancient little chapel. She went back to the car and drove home.

It was four-thirty and, while she had not given Kyle the chance to confirm it, Briony assumed the professor would be coming at seven-thirty for eight, which meant another three hours of staying out of Kyle's way. Without actually sneaking in, she let herself into the house much more quietly than she had left it and gave a startled jump when Kyle unexpectedly opened the drawing-room door and caught her hurrying across the hall.

'Hello, Kyle, you quite startled me.' Briony sped past him with a nervous laugh. 'Vatersay is lovely and I've had a simply super day,' she lied gaily over her shoulder as if the black look on his face had been a pleasant enquiry as to her day. 'I'll be down when the professor arrives,' she called from the top of the stairs and was relieved to hear the restrained slam of the door indicating that Kyle was not about to follow her up.

Shortly after seven she came down to check over the final details with Morag as she usually did, and, as usual, superfluously, since there was nothing Morag loved more than guests at Reef House. The lobster from the local waters and salmon from a farm in one of the bays would be superb, and Morag had already seen to the dining-room, where Briony loitered until she heard the professor's cab pulling up and then joined Kyle in the hall at the very last moment as a final safeguard against any private words he might have had in mind.

She was in her black dress again, and Kyle in jacket and tie; they flicked an appraising eye over each other in silence, and then, with the professor at the door, had no choice but to slip into their roles as host and hostess. After that, it was like any and every other time they had entertained; Kyle was gracious, relaxed, amusing, while she tried to be gracious and made an effort to seem relaxed, but left it to Kyle and Henrik to carry the conversation. Surprisingly, there were quite long stretches at a time when Briony did feel relaxed, when she forgot how things really were between her and Kyle, and that they were just putting on a show for their guest, and found herself enjoying the evening as she used to do in the past.

It was during one of those relaxed stretches and at the end of the meal when Henrik Bergen turned to her and said out of the blue, 'I very much regret that we tourists put you off your visit to the Chille Bharra chapel this afternoon.'

Kyle was looking at her. A vacant little smile glued in place, Briony kept her eyes on their guest and if she had known him better might have tried kicking him under the table.

'This afternoon, Henrik. . .?' Kyle encouraged him with what the professor took for polite interest.

'Yes, this afternoon, Kyle. You see, I had offered to act as guide to a party of American visitors from my hotel,' he began to explain eagerly. 'As you know, I have interested myself in Barra for some years and was most happy to accompany them to explain the history of the chapel and the replica of the runic carved stone displayed there.'

'And you were in Henrik's party, Briony?' Kyle was feigning obtuseness.

'No, Kyle, you have misunderstood me. Miss Hay— Mrs. . . Briony. . .' Henrik Bergen settled upon her name with a diffident smile. 'Briony arrived indepently, but alas, went away again when she saw the chapel overrun with tourists.' He chuckled. 'You did not notice me among them?'

'No. I'm sorry. Shall we go into the drawing-room now?' Her face awash with a warmth she hoped was not showing red in the candlelight, Briony stood up, and, still without meeting Kyle's eyes, led the way out of the room. Outside the drawing-room, her poise recovered a little, she turned to the professor. 'You won't mind if I say goodnight to you now, will you? I'm afraid I have rather a headache, and I'm sure you and Kyle have a lot you'd like to discuss.'

She shook hands, murmured some more pleasantries and would have swept past Kyle with her terse goodnight if he hadn't placed a restraining hand on her arm with the return, 'Goodnight, Briony,' and held her still for a kiss on her mouth.

It was an ordinary light kiss exchanged by any husband and wife in front of people they were comfortable with, and the sort of unselfconscious affection Kyle had displayed in public any number of times throughout their marriage. Tonight's display, though, had just been for show, Briony reminded herself bitterly when the imprint of Kyle's lips on her mouth seemed to linger all the while she prepared for bed. The kiss had been a parody like the entire evening with all its relaxed charm — to which she had succumbed in spite of herself and to which she would probably still be succumbing if the professor hadn't exposed her lie to Kyle — it had been done innocently but had made her feel too embarrassed to stay any longer.

It wasn't Henrik's fault, and Kyle would have found her out sooner or later, because on Barra it was odds on that someone, somewhere would always see you and tell someone else, and she should have borne that in mind and saved herself the hassle of lurking the day away on the other side of the island. Would Kyle say anything about it or leave it be, satisfied in his belief that she had not dared defy him after all, and unaware that she had not intended to go in the first place, and that Martin had not wanted to see hide nor hair of her?

Sitting propped up against the pillows, she was looking out at the teeming rain when Kyle came into the room the next morning, a second after the perfunctory polite rap on the door giving her time to pull the quilt back up to her shoulders. He was in his navy towelling robe, his hair damp from the shower that she had been waiting for him to finish so that she could go in to have hers.

'Headache better?' he asked drily. 'You really must start taking better care of yourself, Briony; that's the second one in as many days.'

Her surly little shrug dislodged the quilt from her shoulders. Briony hastily readjusted it and then flushed at the quizzically raised eyebrow at her display of coyness. The coffee-coloured silk pyjamas were hardly a skimpy négligé, and were long-sleeved ones at that, so it was silly to act as if Kyle had never seen her in them before when he had seen her without them. She started to relax the grip on the quilt, only to retighten it when he came and sat down on the bed beside her, so close that she could feel his thigh against hers through the barrier of the quilt between them, the warmth from his just showered body radiating at her and mingling with the sharp fragrance of soap. Very conscious of the dark spread of hair visible between the top edges of the robe, Briony kept her eyes on his face and her hand determinedly closed over the quilt in case in one unguarded, uncontrollable moment she reached to run her fingers through the familiar soft blackness the way she used to do.

'Why did you lie to me about Martin Gunn and Vatersay?' Kyle's fingers caught her firmly by the chin as she tried to swing her face away, and forced her eyes back to him. 'Were you trying to make me jealous?' he prompted when she wouldn't answer, the soft laugh telling her he had seen right through her. Relaxing his hold, Kyle slid his hand up her cheek and stroked his palm over it in a light caress, watching her with a faint smile as her lips parted slightly in an involuntary reaction to his touch.

'Don't, Kyle,' she protested after the too long moment of letting his hand play its softly sensuous game across her skin, and brought her own agitated hand from the quilt to draw his away from her face, the grapple of fingers ending with both their hands down on the quilt, fingers entwined, and with Kyle still watching her every reaction as he began to tease patterns on her palm with his thumb.

Briony was suddenly very angry. 'The professor isn't here, Kyle,' she pointed out with a bitter little smile.

'What are you talking about?'

'About meaningless displays of affection. Like the public display you put on for Henrik last night. I don't like them.'

'But this is private,' Kyle drawled back softly, sliding his thumb upwards to the sensitive skin of her inner wrist. 'And you do like it.'

Yes, and hated herself for her weakness, because what Kyle was doing had nothing to do with affection. He was playing games, playing on her weakness for him, 'You flatter yourself, Kyle,' she said coldly.

'Do I?' he countered, but was annoyed as he released her hand. 'So why did you lie to me?' The question held curiosity in it this time in place of the smugness she had read into it the first time.

'It wasn't a lie since I fully intended to go,' she lied barefacedly. 'I just happened to change my mind. But I had every right to go if I'd wished. You might still be my husband but I won't accept being ordered about and will do what I please, when I please, and with whom I please.' She spelt out the lie for him and wished it were true — that it really had been the motivation for the dismal day she had inflicted on herself in the attempt to make a gesture — and yes, to try and make Kyle jealous, as he had guessed.

'And haven't you always done exactly that — as you pleased, with whom you pleased?' Kyle challenged, and caught her unprepared with the bitterness in his voice.

Her every muscle seemed to seize instantly into a defensive clench. One more retort, one more sudden twist in the conversation and it would be back to veiled accusations and the open shocking bitterness of no-holds-barred recriminations that she was no more ready for now than she had been on the day of the ceilidh. She shook her head in a series of small jerky shakes, not in denial of his challenge, but in mute appeal.

Kyle ended the tension by abruptly standing up, as if he, too, had recognised what was coming and wanted to back off. He went to the window and watched the rain for a minute or two in silence, and Briony watched him.

'So what do you plan to do with yourself today?' he asked, turning to her.

'Some work, I suppose —— ' She stopped suddenly in anticipation of the usual tensing of the jaw at the mention of her work. But Kyle's expression didn't change; it stayed politely expectant as he waited for her to go on. 'I did some preliminary sketches the other day,' Briony continued after the slight pause, 'and thought I'd get the swatches out of the box still in the boot of my car so I can start deciding about materials.'

'Then you'd better have a fire lit if you're going to be staying upstairs. Do you want one in here or in one of the upstairs rooms, which, I recall, you felt offered the more inspiring view?'

Tartness, mockery she could handle by simply refusing to react to it. 'Upstairs, if it's all the same.'

'Fine. And if you'll give me the key, I can see to your stuff from the boot if you like,' Kyle offered politely.

'Thank you,' said Briony politely too, and those last moments of strained politeness in the bedroom seemed to have set the tone for the day, and the next one, and it was worse than any all-out confrontation or Kyle's subtle sexual overtures.

He did not go out of his way to avoid her, nor did he come looking for her either, and the only time they saw each other were at meals, when he always made a point to ask after her work, and she after his. The carefully courteous conversation of strangers trapped together in a guest house, housebound by the rain and making the best of it — that was how it felt to Briony, and, while Kyle appeared completely unaffected, she thought she would go mad with the strain of talking about their work and the weather, and, in between the meals, working on the collection that had been inspired by, and was evolving entirely around, the woman who had taken Kyle away from her.

It was irony at its most malicious, and the certain knowledge that the Hebridean Collection would be the success that Derek was so obsessed about was a very hollow consolation during the endless hours she spent on it, all the time searingly aware that Kyle was downstairs. And he might as well have been in New York, or she back in London; the distance between them seemed as physical as that, and some-how with more of a finality about it than in that first week of tension and confrontations, of Kyle's and her own anger, and of those flashes of unchecked sexual desire for each other.

Had they really happened? Sitting across the dinner-table from Kyle and making polite conver-sation, Briony wondered if she hadn't just imagined them, and then sometimes, when she turned her head unexpectedly and found Kyle watching her with that unfathomable expression in his eyes, she won-dered whether he wasn't wondering exactly the same thing.

Tuesday morning brought blue skies again and sun with warmth in it. From her bedroom window, she looked down the slope dipping from the house to the water and watched Kyle walking up and down the shore as he must have watched her from his study window. There was still a light breeze left after the wind of the last two days, and it was tossing Kyle's hair about so that the black strands glinted blue as they lifted and caught the sun. Hands in pockets, he strode on, in his element and loving it, and in that moment Briony felt more alienated from him, more excluded from his life than ever she had in those first months after he had left her.

'Would you like to come to the tatties and herring evening tonight?' Kyle asked when they were break-fasting a little later.

Asking her to go out with him. . .? The next thought flashed in the night of the ceilidh, and Ishabel, and stopped the spark of pleasure in its tracks. 'A theme dinner evening like the haggis evening we went to last year, do you mean?' Briony played for time with her own question instead of answering his.

'When you came face to face with a haggis and your good manners won the day? That's right, very similar to that.' Kyle reminded her wryly of her brave attempt to meet the challenge sitting on her plate that evening.

Briony couldn't help the spontaneous laugh. 'It wasn't nearly as bad as I thought it would be, and I did love the piping-in-the-haggis ceremony beforehand.'

'But wouldn't care to repeat the culinary part of the exercise for another decade or two?' Kyle smiled. 'Anyway, it's *buntata agus sgadan* this year, and I know you've liked the dish when Morag has served it. Besides, we could do with a change from being cooped up in the house.'

Cooped up with her when he could be with some-body else? Briony fought the question she knew she was powerless to stop. 'Will. . . Henrik be there?' The substitution of name was only giving herself a temporary reprieve.

'I doubt if there's been a Feis function to date that Henrik hasn't braved rain and gales to attend. He's interested in positively everything from piping eve-nings to cockle-gathering to Gaelic lessons, which I believe he's taking. Yes, he will very definitely be there this evening,' Kyle confirmed with a dry chuckle at his friend's passion for anything remotely Gaelic.

It was not the professor's activities that she was interested in. 'Will Ishabel be there tonight. . .?' Briony had a vague hope of the question passing for casual, a vain hope she realised when the words came out as if they were choking her. She forced herself to keep her eyes on Kyle's face and watched the last of his amusement fade without a trace, watched for signs of tension — guilt — and saw nothing except a po-faced impassiveness. Kyle had always been an excellent poker player.

'I expect so,' he replied carelessly, and, unlike her, managed the casualness without a bat of an eye. 'Along with about another hundred people,' he added, with a faint quirk of a smile.

'Thank you, no. I mean, it all sounds very nice,' Briony put in, terribly graciously,' 'but I won't go, thank you all the same. I'm afraid that I——'

'I won't accept a headache without a doctor's certificate, Briony, if you're thinking of having another one this evening.' After two days of absence, the edge was all at once back in Kyle's voice, and the smile just his white, very even teeth on show.

Briony showed her own in a mocking smile. 'I was under the impression that you were asking me, and that it was up to me to decide whether or not I wanted to accept your invitation, but I do take it that you are actually insisting that I come with you this evening?'

'I was asking, but, if you prefer, yes, I could very easily change it to insisting,' Kyle said with ominous pleasantness, and jolted an involuntary, shocked laugh out of her at his absurd, arrogant belief that he had a right to insist she do anything, or go anywhere with him.

'Honestly, Kyle, sometimes I think you forget which century you're living in. Yes, Morag, we've quite finished.' She switched her gaze to the old lady as she came into the breakfast-room wearing the pleased, knowing look which had become her standard expression whenever she saw them together now — a look that annoyed Briony no end, based as it was on Morag's misreading of the domestic scene that was nothing more than façade.

'And will you be staying in for dinner tonight, my dears?' Morag smiled warmly at them as she started to clear the table.

Briony flicked her eyes to Kyle and back to Morag. 'No. Kyle and I will be going to the tatties and herring evening,' she told the housekeeper, and Kyle.

What else could she do? Briony asked herself for the umpteenth time as she waited for Kyle down in the hall that evening to avoid any possibility of a repetition of the pre-ceilidh scene in the bedroom. Short of bodily carrying her there, Kyle couldn't actually force her to go, and why he was so adamant that she should go Briony couldn't fathom, but if she changed her mind now and refused to go he would simply go without her and it was a moot point as to which would be the more unbearable: staying away and picturing Kyle with Ishabel, or going and seeing him with Ishabel.

'Have I kept you waiting?' Kyle came around the curve of the last flight of stairs and looked surprised to see her hovering edgily by the door in a reversal of their roles of their last night out together.

'Oh, no. No, I was just ready early and had some things to do down here,' Briony lied in the catch of breath at how fantastic Kyle looked in the dark navy suit which set off the hard, dark edge about him that she sometimes found so threatening, and always so very attractive — like a drug addict, she thought, quite shocked by her own analogy. Like someone who was addicted to something she knew to be dangerous, but who couldn't stop herself, and who really didn't want to be cured of her addiction at all.

'You look beautiful.' Kyle took his time over the lingering appraisal of the black and white silk. . . simple, elegant, beautifully cut with long sleeves and with the V of the front low, but not so low as to be blatantly sexy. Her hair was caught back at the nape again and her shoes flat for Castlebay's slopes and the Eightsome Reel.

'Thank you,' Briony murmured self-consciously, annoyed with herself for the moment of reading too much into the admiration in Kyle's eyes. . .for being too desperately on the look-out for signs, while at the same time afraid of them because she knew they wouldn't mean what she wanted them to mean. And afraid that in the end she simply might not care and accept whatever little Kyle was prepared to offer her before she left.

CHAPTER EIGHT

ISHABEL MACLEOD was nowhere in sight. That was the first thing Briony noted in her sweep of an eye over the small hall, and then continued noting as Kyle took her around from one group of people to the next, some standing, some already seated at the large tables down two walls of the hall.

His arm had settled around her waist as they made their entrance, and stayed there, casually — naturally, it must have looked to everybody they talked to, and only Briony knew that it was just to project a public show of togetherness: the appearance that all was well with the Buchanans. But whatever Kyle's reason she was glad of his arm around her, for its reassurance, because she had been more nervous than she realised of taking her place among the islanders again . . .resuming her 'place', albeit temporarily, as Kyle's wife.

The island's social activities started late in summer, some as late as ten, and, while this one was scheduled for nine, it was well past nine-thirty by the time everybody was finally seated. And still there was no sign of Ishabel. Briony's fears of another strained, if not humiliating evening dissolved in a flood of relief which, after the build-up of tension, made her quite light-headed as she relaxed and stopped looking towards the door every time there was any movement near it.

'I've missed this,' she told Kyle with a genuinely happy smile, the gesture of her hand indicating the kilted piper at the far end who had just finished the first of his pieces of the evening, but really meaning everybody and everything in the little hall. . .the familiar faces around the tables. . .the cheerful comfortableness of the informal island gathering where everybody knew everybody else and evenings like this had the air of a large family get-together.

Of the people at their table, only the teacher and his wife were strangers; the rest she knew. . . Peter, one of the Feis organisers, his wife Fiona, her brother Iain. And dear old Henrik Bergen beside her, immediately filling her in on everything he had attended and done since their last meeting at Reef House. In her new, relaxed mood, Briony was quite prepared to find him fascinating.

'I'm starving,' she was laughingly saying to him as the first of the women from the kitchen emerged bearing plates and filling the hall with the instantly recognisable fragrance of the steaming combination of potatoes and herrings. 'It's so long since I've —— '

An apron over a dusky pink dress and a tray in her hands, Ishabel Macleod was following a middle-aged woman out of the kitchen, and looking not very pleased about it.

Ishabel serving the food? Briony's first reaction was astonishment; after it came the quick oblique glance at Kyle talking to the teacher's wife on his other side, and not yet aware of Ishabel. Then came her tension and the awful compulsion to follow the girl's every step as Ishabel attended to a table across the hall.

'Ah, yes, the very lovely Miss Macleod.' The professor had not failed to notice the focus of her eyes and attention. 'Her father is the proprietor of the hotel I am staying in, and I believe is responsible for the catering here this evening. Kyle has also told me he is the island's best chess player and I am very much hoping for a game with him before I leave Barra.'

'Oh,' said Briony and darted another glance at Kyle, looking across the hall now but showing no surprise to see Ishabel waitressing.

Not on their table, though; she didn't come near them, whether deliberately or not Briony had no way of knowing. All she hoped was that it would be like that for the rest of the evening but knew in her heart that the girl wouldn't be able to stay away from Kyle — and she was right.

Apron off, and flushed pink above the dusky pink of her dress, Ishabel joined their table after the second of the noisy whirling reels which always started off the after-dinner dancing, and which had left Briony as flushed as Ishabel, and almost breathless after the unaccustomed exercise. She had returned to her place with Henrik, who had, amazingly, kicked up his heels with the best of them, but in the general switch of places Kyle ended up facing her across the table and it was Andrew, the schoolteacher, who was now sitting next to her, while Ishabel was between Kyle and Peter. In the circumstances Briony did not expect the girl to ignore her as she had on the two previous occasions, but wasn't prepared for the naturalness of the smile.

'Hello, Miss Hayward, it's nice to see you again,'

Ishabel greeted her with no sign of embarrassment, and seemed perfectly at ease sitting next to Kyle with his wife directly opposite her.

Briony put down her glass of wine, murmured something indistinct through a forced smile and willed herself not to look at Kyle, while at the same time sensed that Kyle was willing her to look at him. Challenging her to look at him, it felt like, and when she couldn't hold out any longer he was ready with a small curve of smile in place as their eyes made the glancing contact. Briony swerved hers away instantly and determinedly didn't look at him again.

Andrew was trying to talk above the background of music and the laughter of the dancers behind Kyle and Ishabel who had their backs to the floor; Briony tried to listen and every now and then caught snatches of Ishabel's voice as well. The girl was speaking to Kyle in Gaelic; Briony couldn't hear Kyle at all. She gave up straining to hear, or listening to Andrew, and sipped her wine grimly instead, and when the music and dancing stopped Henrik was the only one talking. His voice, which had been raised to counter the music, was over-loud now as he finished giving Peter across the table an account of his trip to Mingulay. Briony had heard it before, in great detail.

'I've heard it's very lovely but haven't been there myself yet,' Ishabel said wistfully to Kyle, and to Briony the accompanying hand on his arm made it look and sound like a request to be taken there — by Kyle.

'Haven't you?' She joined the conversation in a bright little burst. 'Oh, Kyle and I have often been over there. In fact, we're planning another trip as soon as we've both got a spare minute, aren't we, Kyle?' Had she really sung that out? She must have because everybody was looking at her, and Briony felt as embarrassed as if she'd just shouted, Get your hand off my husband, at the top of her voice.

It had been a rhetorical, throwaway sort of question but in the pause in the conversation that followed it everybody seemed to be waiting politely for Kyle's reply before they resumed talking. Her heart pounding, Briony made herself turn to him too, and in that long look across the table felt, as their eyes locked, that they were the only people in the room.

'Yes, we are,' Kyle finally confirmed, lightly, and with one of his funny twists of smile, and then everybody started to talk again at once. In embarrassment. . .? Had they guessed that she had put Kyle on the spot? Or in relief that he had backed up her lie?

Briony picked up her wine again, aware that she was drinking too much—her fourth. . .fifth. . .? She had lost count, but, however many it was, it was probably too many. Out of the corner of her eye, she could see Kyle looking at her. Disapprovingly. . .? Without looking directly back at him she couldn't tell, but suspected it was. Defiantly almost, she finished the glass and was tempted to ask Henrik to pour her another only she was not so tipsy that she didn't realise that the lethal combination of tension and alcohol had embarrassed her quite enough already. Drained her, too, and all she really wanted was to go home. It was late and the boisterous reel music had given way to slow old-time dance music signalling the winding down of the evening.

'Excuse me, please, Henrik,' she murmured as she picked up her bag and stood up before he decided to ask her to join the couples on the floor. Or before Kyle and Ishabel joined them.

Kyle had stood up too, to draw Ishabel to her feet for a dance, Briony thought, but as she went to go past him he took the bag from her and put it on the table.

'Excuse us,' he said to the table in general, led her on to the floor and took her into his arms, not in a polite dancing hold, but drawn into himself very closely in what was virtually an embrace to music, in public.

Only a few couples were dancing; the rest were seated, watching, and in the beginning Briony was very conscious of everybody's eyes on them. And then she was conscious only of Kyle, his cheek against hers, his hand low and warm on her back. . . conscious of his body as it guided her slowly around the little hall, all the time moulding her closer and closer and sending her every nerve haywire. As always.

It was the way they had first danced—moved sensuously to music among the ferns and flowers in the conservatory on the night they had met—and although they had danced together many times after that, on Barra as well as during their time in London, it was that very first time in Kyle's arms that her body was remembering now and melting into turbulence. A contradiction in terms, but that was how it felt as Briony let herself slide into the whirlpool of sensation.

When the dance was over Kyle eased them apart,

reluctantly. 'I think we ought to go home now, don't you?' he murmured, and her body, still in its time-warp, heard a promise in the voice, and suggestion, and reacted with a sudden spasm of anticipation somewhere low and deep inside.

She nodded.

Ishabel was no longer at their table. Briony freed herself from the arm around her waist and picked up her bag. 'I won't be long,' she murmured, and headed to the Ladies', needing to put some physical distance between them, if only for a few minutes, to give her body time to pull itself together.

The group of girls made room for her at the mirror. Moving to it to touch up her lipstick, she saw herself as Kyle had seen her a few moments ago. . .eyes lustrous, skin softly flushed and very warm to the touch when she put a palm experimentally against her cheek. The wine, Briony told herself, and knew she was lying. Finishing quickly at the mirror, and with a 'goodnight' to no one in particular, she was nearly at the door when it swung open and Ishabel walked in. 'Goodnight, Ishabel,' she said stiffly as she went past.

'Goodbye, Miss Hayward,' Ishabel replied pleasantly.

'Mrs Buchanan, actually,' Briony corrected sharply over her shoulder but it was the pointed 'goodbye' instead of 'goodnight' that really cata-pulted her out of the lingering warm sensation of Kyle's arms still around her and back into cold reality. If Ishabel knew she was leaving it could only be because Kyle had told her and it was small wonder that the girl could act pleasantly, knowing as she did that the Buchanans' display of togetherness was a sham, and a very temporary one — a fact Briony's body had tricked her mind into blocking out during that sensuous, almost private dance. Angry with herself, she swept out into the hall where Kyle was standing near their table in a group with a ready-to-leave air about it.

'Here she is, so you can ask her yourself,' he said to Peter as she joined them and he reached out a hand as if to slip it around her waist.

Pretending not to notice it, Briony stepped out of range. 'Ask me what?' She looked at Peter questioningly.

'Whether you'd be agreeable to giving out some of the prizes at the games on Sunday?'

'Me?' The moment of spontaneous pleasure at being asked was cancelled the next instant by the realisation that she wouldn't be here. 'But I ——' She turned to Kyle in confusion.

'Perhaps Briony can give you a ring about it in the next day or so?' Kyle suggested casually.

'Fine. I've rather sprung it on you, I know, but it would be a great help if you could manage it. Anyway, let me know by Friday if you can,' Peter added as they all moved towards the door and out into the car park, Briony walking on ahead with his wife to keep herself still out of range of Kyle's arm. The show was over as far as she was concerned.

'Why didn't you tell him that I'll be leaving on Thursday?' she finally asked in the car, breaking the silence that was threatening to last all the way home.

'Why didn't you?' Kyle countered.

Why hadn't she? Her own reluctance was as

incomprehensible as Kyle's. 'I. . . I didn't want to disappoint Peter outright,' she said lamely. 'But of course I can't do it—stay until Sunday.' The uncertain little inflexion almost turned the statement into a question.

'It's up to you.' Kyle kept his eyes on the road.

Up to her to extend her stay to continue the charade? Was that what Kyle meant. . . Wanted? With a small sigh of frustration Briony gave up trying to decipher the give-nothing-away profile, settled her head back against the seat and closed her eyes.

'Not another headache?'

Mocking or teasing? Whichever, she interpreted it as a comment on her drinking and snapped her eyes open. 'I'm tired, that's all. And if you're implying that I was drinking too much I wasn't. I was just enjoying myself,' she defended herself with the piqued lie.

'I'm glad to hear it. I was too—enjoying myself.'

Watching the suppressed hostility of two women who were both crazy about him? Playing one off against the other. . .? How could she tell what Kyle had been enjoying or what he was about any more? Briony lapsed into silence for the rest of the way and didn't wait while he parked the car but got out at the door and went straight into the house and upstairs, then heard him go into his study as she went into the bathroom to take off her make-up and get ready for bed.

She felt very, very tired—of everything. . .the expectations, hopes, which could still be set off by something as meaningless as an admiring look or a four-minute dance; of her own persistent delusions

that some miracle could yet save her marriage — a
marriage she had not realised needed saving until it
was too late. And she was tired of Kyle playing
confusing games with her feelings in public shows of
affection which this evening had fooled the locals —
and her too, briefly — into believing she was still part
of his life, and of the island's. Why else had Peter
asked her to help out with the prize-giving? A
compliment, yes, but with an edge since it was Kyle
Buchanan's wife he had asked, not Briony Hayward.

Yet it wouldn't hurt to stay and help him out. Help
Peter. . .? Who was she kidding? Briony mocked
herself wryly. If she stayed it would be for the extra
days with Kyle, days of strain and more talk about
their work and the weather, or with Kyle's unpredictability, perhaps yet more furious confrontations. It
was madness even to think she could put herself
through it.

The slam of a door woke her from the deep sleep;
a car door, Briony hazily distinguished, and, listening
for the growl of engine, heard feet up the stairs
instead and jerked to a sitting position a second
before Kyle strode in.

Dressed in jeans and a black T-shirt, he had a
briskness — an impatience — about him. 'Good morning. You're awake. Good,' he said crisply from just
inside the door. 'I've organised everything so we can
be off as soon as you're ready.'

Briony stared, blankly.

'To Mingulay.'

'Minuglay? Today? Now. . .?'

'I happen to have a spare minute if you have.'

Her own words sounded mortifyingly idiotic but

must have sounded a lot worse last night when she had trilled them across the table at Ishabel.

'You do want to go?' Kyle smiled tart enjoyment as he put her on the spot, as she had him.

Did she — want to go. . .? Actually going to Mingulay had not entered her mind last night, but now. . .? Forced into a decision, Briony realised that yes, she did want to go; she did want to make a last trip to the tiny island which she and Kyle had visited each of the previous three summers.

She nodded slowly. 'Yes, I'd very much like to visit Mingulay again.'

'Good.' Kyle gave one of his abrupt laughs that she couldn't fathom. 'The boat leaves at eleven. It's after nine now. Take something warm; you know how changeable the weather can be.'

'Yes, all right,' she agreed, frowning and completely at a loss as to why Kyle should be putting himself out to make good her lie when surely just backing her up had been enough for appearances' sake. Appearances as they applied to her, not to Kyle, of course. . .so absolutely, arrogantly sure of himself and his position on the island that he could do whatever he chose with whomever he chose and no one would ever question it.

He had already packed the car. Briony cast a startled eye at the mountain of stuff taking up most of the back of it. . .an enormous hamper, rugs, waterproof jackets, and heaven only knew what else. 'If everybody turns up with what we're taking, Seumas will need to tow along a second boat to fit us all in.'

Kyle laughed as if she had made a joke, and

Morag, hovering at the passenger-side window, murmured worriedly that she hoped she had packed in
enough food, and told them to be careful not to
catch cold. When the forecast was twenty-three
degrees. . .? Briony assured her that they would do
their best to stay warm.

'Are you sure you haven't overlooked anything?'
she asked Kyle facetiously. 'All we need are the
boots and rucksacks and we'd pass for birdwatchers.'

Their previous cruises had been in the company of
about two dozen tourists, mainly avid birdwatchers
whose indefatigable pursuit to sight whichever species drove their particular passion took them from
the bird colony of St Kilda in the Hebridean north to
Mingulay in the south, and when Kyle pulled up at
the pier in Castlebay Briony expected to see the
hardy booted and rucksacked contingent already
waiting.

The pier was deserted of birdwatchers, and of
tourists altogether, and only some fishermen were
unloading their catch off one of the trawlers.

'But where is everybody?' She turned to Kyle in
puzzlement after he had unloaded the car and given
the key to one of the fishermen to drive it back up
the Street to park later.

'Who?'

'The birdwatchers — tourists, for the cruise.'

'There isn't any cruise on today. Seumus is running
us over in his outboard-motor boat,' Kyle explained
with a casualness at variance with the watchfulness
in his eyes as he took in her new surprise.

'Just us?' In a mad moment of paranoid suspicion
Briony flung a wild look towards the Street, fully

expecting to see Ishabel Macleod gliding towards them to join the excursion.

'Just us,' Kyle confirmed, still watching her carefully. 'And I rather think it might be a pleasant change to be able to wander about without tripping over a birdwatcher lying in wait at every rabbit burrow for a puffin to pop out.'

'Yes. . .yes, I suppose so,' Briony murmured uneasily, and felt more than just a little discomfited that Kyle had apparently organised this trip especially for her. For them.

'Do you want to change your mind and not go?' He offered her the last-minute option even as Seumas was putting their gear into the boat.

She glanced at the boat and back at Kyle, then laughed edgily. 'No, of course I don't. Why should I?' she countered airily, and could have come up with any number of reasons, not least of which was the instant knot of tension inside her already at the propect of being alone with Kyle.

Once on the boat, however, she began to relax. It would have been impossible not to. The route had lost none of its magic as they skirted tiny islands once upon a time occupied by a few families or the odd hermit. . .past outcrops of rocks covered with sun-bathing seals, and their every mile accompanied by sea birds swooping overhead or bobbing around in the sparkling green water. By the time the awesome sheer cliffs of Mingulay loomed into sight just over an hour later, Briony had almost slipped into a captivating time-warp, and had to remind herself that the man beside her, looking on smiling and perhaps even sharing her enjoyment as she pointed out this and that along the way, was not the Kyle of their previous trips, but the confusing, arrogant Kyle she didn't know any more, and who would revert to being that incomprehensible stranger as soon as they returned to Reef House.

CHAPTER NINE

WITH no natural harbour, landing on Mingulay was a precarious business—impossible in winter, and, even now when Seumus could run the small boat almost to the edge of the sand of the cove on the gentler side of the island, it was still a protracted hassle to get themselves and their gear off the boat and up the beach.

A deserted beach on an abandoned island.

It felt like the end of the earth. The most beautiful end of the earth imaginable, and she and Kyle its only, temporary inhabitants. And what were they doing here? Alone? With Seumus and the boat gone, Briony's unease resurfaced and set in in the form of an over-awareness of Kyle at her side as they wandered about the sad remains of the village, in ruins except for the old priest house, and abandoned to the birds and rabbits, and sheep brought over to graze from Barra.

Every time he took her hand to help her up the slope above the village, or down again, she was acutely, intensely conscious of him, physically. . .of her own growing tension and the sense of expectancy, or was it expectation. . .that he would take her in his arms in the all-resolving cliché of romantic fantasy and tell her that he'd brought her to this magical island to make love to her? That he couldn't stand their estrangement any longer?

The enchanting setting must have turned her head. Kyle was as pleasant and chatty as a paid guide, and, for all the intermittent hand-holding, just as courteously aloof as he had been during their two days of being housebound by the rain. In the circumstances, her tension seemed ridiculous as they carried the rugs and hamper to the grassy slope above the village from where they could look across to Berneray, the very last island of the Hebridean archipelago, and uninhabited too, since the lighthouse went automatic.

'I think Morag had in mind she was catering for a boatload of starving tourists.' Briony studied the hamper in astonishment, crammed as it was with what must have been half the contents of Reef House's pantry. . .salmon, cold meats, boiled eggs, bread, fruit and even several bottles of white wine among the flasks of coffee.

'You know our Morag,' Kyle smiled, unsurprised.

Yes, she did, and knew the darling old lady had gone overboard—not just with the food, but in her expectations for the afternoon—a romantic afternoon, if the wine was any indication. Expectations no more absurd than her own. . .had been, Briony thought sadly, as later she watched Kyle wandering up and down the beach. Looking out for Seumus already. . .?

She had dozed off. When she opened her eyes it was to look straight into Kyle's. His shirt off, he was propped up on an elbow beside her on the rug, leaning over her slightly, and when he smiled the reach of her hand to his face was completely spontaneous, something so natural to her whenever she woke to find Kyle watching over her that she had already caressed her fingertips down his cheek and was following the familiar hard angles of his jawline before she realised what she was doing. Her hand became stock-still in that moment of surprise, and then for endless moments more it seemed as if they were both holding their breath while they waited to see what she would do next.

Very deliberately, and with her eyes locked with Kyle's, Briony resumed the slow caressing path over his face, finishing the sensuous journey the way she had always done, with the delicate tracing of a fingertip over the outline of his lips, and knew exactly what she was doing and what Kyle would take it to mean. With nothing changed between them, and no more guarantee of reconciliation than there had been on that shattering evening of the ceilidh, she was now telling him she wanted him, asking him to make love to her as openly as if she were putting it into words.

'Kyle. . .?' She dropped her hand from his face.

'No words, *mo ghràdh*.' He bent his head to her swiftly so that his own words came as a soft explosion of warm moist breath into her mouth and as part of the kiss itself.

Briony closed her eyes on the wave of relief and surrendered her mouth to the gently probing tongue that was making no demands, yet conveying the promise that they would come and that she would love them. She could feel the same promise in the restrained hand that lay deliberately heavy on the flatness of her jean-covered abdomen, and in its slow upward meander to her breasts, over them, but staying outside the shirt and not venturing inside it, as if the reassurance of the familiar shape beneath was all that Kyle wanted or needed for the moment. Her own hands swept much more urgently over the tautly muscled shoulders, smooth and sun-warmed, and even his hair held the same warmth when she laced her fingers through the thick black waves in increasing agitation before drawing his head down harder to intensify the pressure of the kiss.

Kyle was easing off the savouring of her mouth gradually, but much too soon, and, while she tried to delay the final moment as long as she could by refusing to release his mouth, in the end Kyle forcefully drew her hands down and his mouth away.

'Briony, *m'eudail*, I adore the taste of your mouth but it's not enough,' Kyle groaned desperately, his hands at the buttons of her shirt even as he was drawing her to her feet to undress her.

Undressed already by his eyes, and incited by his need to touch her, to look at her, Briony turned their fingers into a tangle in her trembling haste to help him. Then all at once she stopped, and the next instant was trying to peel his hands away from her.

'No, Kyle,' she protested, and only realised how she had sounded and what Kyle had thought she meant by it when he swung his eyes up to her face in shocked disbelief. 'Oh, God, no, I didn't mean that. I meant about Seumus, the boat. When is Seumus due?' she clarified urgently.

'Three-thirty,' Kyle told her after the short jolt of unamused laughter at his own shock, and brought his hand up to flick a glance at his watch. 'Five-fifteen,' he answered before she asked.

'But that means. . .'

'That he should have been here nearly two hours ago, yes,' he finished for her without any sign of concern. 'It's nothing to worry about. At a guess I'd say he's made some sort of mistake about the prevailing currents this afternoon. You know what they're like around these parts.'

Briony didn't have a clue. She shook her head.

'It just means Seumus won't be able to get back here until tomorrow, that's all.'

'Oh!' Her surprise melted into relief, then pleasure in the space of that small exclamation.

'You don't mind, do you?' Kyle smiled the question, a token one since her face could not have left him in any doubt about how she felt about the prospect of a night alone with him on Mingulay, and Kyle was not interested in any answer but that from her body to each new caress of his hands and mouth as he undressed her, slowly, holding back his urgency to heighten the anticipation — hers, as well as his own.

It was erotic foreplay in slow motion with each new curve which was uncovered being shaped and stroked by Kyle's hands and teased into piercing, throbbing response by his tongue. Aroused unbearably by the time they were both naked, she was trembling from her excitement as Kyle released her hair from its clasp and threaded his fingers through it to lift and sift and spread it over her shoulders while all the time the darkly burning eyes adored her like some golden goddess from the myths of his island's Viking past.

'I've been going insane waiting for this,' he told

her harshly, suddenly pulling her to him to engulf her in his arms. His face buried in the curve of her neck, he just held her against his aroused, bruisingly hard body as if he wanted to leave an imprint of himself on her forever.

He had already done that long ago—claimed her as his own—and now when he eased them down on to the rug again it was to reclaim her, every part of her, with an urgent possessiveness in his hands and mouth as they travelled inexorably up and down her body to stroke and kiss and taste all over again, no longer tantalising or teasing responses from her, but demanding them with a ruthless insistence that spun her senses and her body into turmoil.

Yet each abandoned cry wrought from her was not enough for Kyle at her breasts, or down between the silky smoothness of her thighs, until she was clinging to him in a tumult of sensations that were beyond pleasure, her uncontrollable cries reverberating around the island and indistinguishable from the wild cries of the birds as she arched and tossed, and then drew him up frantically to put an end to the exquisite torment with the final act of possession.

'Kyle, please. . .*Tha gaol agam ort.*'

'Again. Tell me again,' Kyle ordered in his own harsh anguish.

'*Tha goal agam ort. Is tu mo ghràdh.* I love you,' she kept repeating in both languages as Kyle entered her, and she was aware of his gasp at the shock of his own pleasure as he became part of her at last, covering her with his body and blocking out the light. All she could see was his face, the blackness of his head a dark shadow against the blue and gold blur behind him. All she could feel were the thrusts of his body reaching into the very core of her being and her whole world was Kyle, and she his, in those last moments when they cried out each other's name.

Afterwards, she lay curved into his body, Kyle's arm around her, and wondered how she could have held back from him last week when he had wanted her, why she had let her own doubts and the shadow of Ishabel Macleod continue to threaten the chance of a reconciliation between them. Briony gave an involuntary shiver and snuggled closer into Kyle's side, gazing up at him as she twined her fingers through the soft black spread of hair over his chest and then followed its tapering path downwards, watching his eyes darken with pleasure as she shaped her hand over him and feeling a corresponding thrill of pleasure and almost of triumph that she could elicit that look of ecstasy, the passionate response, and later the renewed cries of love that she had been so afraid she would never hear again.

They fell asleep in each other's arms under a rug and the cloak of semi-darkness which covered the island and the sea. When she woke to the brightness of morning, she was alone. Disorientated, Briony sat up, irrationally alarmed until she saw Kyle in the water just in from the shore, and then she laughed aloud at her own instant of panic that he was gone from her.

She watched him for a while, just loving the sight of him, then wanted to be with him, and, slipping on her knickers with just the shirt over them, made her way across the grassy dune and over the sand to the edge of the water.

'Come on, come in to me,' Kyle called to her as she stood with her feet in the ice-cold shallows, unwarmed by the sun yet and never really warm at any time of day, any time of year.

She shook her head smilingly. 'No, I'll wait for you out here.' She walked back up the sand to settle herself on the rug Kyle had left beside a towel and his bundle of clothes.

He was a good swimmer and enjoyed the water, whereas she had an irrational fear of it. Briony watched the powerful play of muscles as his shoulders caught the light in each forceful stroke through the translucent green water. . .watched him coming out of the water and towards her, felt her stomach go into a clench with the catch of breath and wondered how any man who looked as wonderful as Kyle could be so utterly indifferent to his looks and the body he so invariably clothed so carelessly.

Looking at the hard, lean naked body now it was obvious why Kyle had no interest in clothes. He simply didn't need to. His body was strong enough, vital enough to speak for itself under whatever dark 'uniform' he chose to toss over it, unlike people— men as well as women—who needed clothes to enhance their personalities as much as their bodies. No one knew that better than she did, with her dealings with models, some extraordinarily beautiful yet with about as much personality as coldly beautiful statues.

Like Ishabel Macleod, Briony suddenly thought, and wished she hadn't.

Reaching her, Kyle picked up the towel and gave

himself a brisk rub down before wrapping it around
his waist and lowering himself beside her.

'Good morning, *m'eudail*.'

His mouth tasted of the sea and the tang of it was
in his wet hair and radiating from his body when he
pulled her closer to himself in the kiss that had so
much hunger in it that their mouths might have been
separated for months, not just a few hours.

'I'm starved for you again already,' Kyle told her
with a soft laugh when he broke off the kiss so that
they could catch their breath.

And she for him. Briony let her hands linger
around his face, loving the scratchy roughness against
her palms as she slid them caressingly over the dark
stubble which she had not seen for so long—and had
missed. . .even that, like everything else about him.

Kyle drew her hands down from his face. 'You'll
scratch yourself, darling.' He ran his own palm in a
quick check over his cheek and grimaced. 'I didn't
think to bring along my shaving gear. I'm sorry.'

Briony burst out laughing. 'I shouldn't imagine
many men would when they're setting out for an
afternoon's sail. Kyle, do put on your T-shirt; it's not
warm enough yet for sunbathing,' she ordered—like
a concerned wife—and loved the sound of herself.

Smiling, Kyle did as he was told and pulled the
black T-shirt over his head. 'Is that better? What was
it you were thinking about when I was coming up
along the sand?' he asked, curious. 'You seemed so
. . .oddly distant—looking at me and not seeing me,
it felt like.'

'I saw you,' she assured him with a laugh.

'That's a relief. I thought for a moment that I'd

become invisible.' Kyle propped himself on his elbow and stretched out his frame alongside her. 'So what were you thinking?' he persisted.

'Nothing very much, just about bodies and clothes, and how some people need clothes and some don't — you know. . .to give them personalities, that sort of thing,' Briony clarified a little self-consciously under his frankly interested gaze. 'Of course some women are so beautiful they don't need either the clothes or the personalities to be desirable, do they?' she heard herself adding in a helpless, uncontrollable aside, and could have died. She swung her face quickly from him to the water.

'Women like?'

Briony stayed silent.

'Like. . .?' Kyle prompted again insistently and eased himself up off his elbow to a sitting position.

'Women like Ishabel Macleod,' Briony said finally, dully, still without looking at him, and seized into knots inside. Her arms wrapped tightly around her knees, she kept staring ahead at the water, too afraid to look at him until Kyle put a hand under her chin and turned her face to him again.

'Are you trying to bring yourself to ask me if I've been having an affair with Ishabel?' he asked very evenly, and read her answer in her eyes. He dropped his hand from her face. 'Are you sure, *m'eudail*, that you want to talk about this now?' It was a funny sort of smile. . .soft and faintly bitter, and with something akin to a dare in it, and in his voice too. 'Because it's not going to be just a simple matter of my saying yes or no, is it?'

Briony thought she understood what he meant,

and no, it would not be a simple matter, but the start of an endless flowchart. . .if yes, then move to the box marked 'hurt', and then on to the whys and wherefores; if no. . . But it wouldn't be a no because then it would have been simple for Kyle to say it, to reassure her that her fears had been groundless — or at least were groundless now. But surely she knew that herself? Kyle had told her — shown her in a way that should not have left her in any doubt — how much he loved her. Wasn't that reassurance enough? It had to be.

Her answer to his questions was an impulsive, sudden reach to him to curve her arms around his neck. 'Make love to me again, Kyle. Please.' Reassure me again, she meant.

Seumus came at three-thirty. 'On the dot — give or take twenty-four hours,' Briony laughed as they watched the small boat's approach, and she heaped mental blessings on the boatman's head for his miscalculation — or whatever — of the Hebridean currents.

She gave him a positively radiant smile as, jeans soaked to the knees, she clambered, was hauled, pushed, into the boat. 'Hello, Seumus, I hope you didn't worry about us. We were quite safe.'

'I'm sure you were, Mrs Buchanan, since I've not recently heard of anybody being nibbled to death by rabbits on Mingulay,' Seumus chuckled, and kept up an intermittent chuckling at his own corny witticism long after he had rounded the cliffs of Mingulay.

Sitting close in to Kyle's side, his arm around her, Briony watched the magical, lonely island recede into a dot in the blue distance and felt as happy as she had ever been in her life. Kyle was hers again; she was in love with her own husband and didn't care who knew it. . . Seumus with his kindly, knowing smiles in between the chuckling; the fishermen on the pier back in Castlebay; people in the Street when they went to get the car to bring it back to the pier to collect their gear.

Morag sized up the situation in one sharp flick of the dark currant eyes when they returned to Reef House. Then she broke into a smile that was as knowing as ever but relieved too, and, most of all, happy.

'You weren't worried about us, Morag, were you?' Briony asked as the old lady helped to take the things out of the car.

'Och, no, lass. But did you have enough food to last you?'

'For a week, thank you,' Briony assured her solemnly as she exchanged smiles with Kyle.

'But you can't have eaten a thing. My hamper looked barely touched.' Morag tut-tutted in admonishment later when Briony came down into the kitchen. 'And you shouldn't be walking about with damp hair like that; you'll get an earache,' she added with a disapproving frown at Briony's just washed and towel-dried hair.

'We've only just finished our shower.' Ridiculously, Briony suddenly blushed, as if the housekeeper had never heard of a man and woman showering together.

Morag's eyes twinkled. 'I'll make you a cup of tea

now, shall I, before I start on dinner? You'll be staying in tonight, will you not?'

'Yes.'

'And you'll not be leaving again, will you, *m'eudail*?' Abruptly, Morag reached a hand to her cheek and gave it an affectionate little pat.

'I have to, Morag, and probably as early as the end of next week. Only for a couple of weeks—just to start winding up my business in London.' She explained what she had not yet explained to Kyle because somehow the right moment had not yet come up. Neither of them had mentioned the ferry she had missed today, but her return to London— however temporary—couldn't be put off indefinitely, and what Briony was hoping was that Kyle would want to come with her so that they did not need to be separated again. 'What is it, Morag?'

Morag's mouth had frozen into a startled 'Oh'.

'Och, my memory is like a sieve. You mentioning your business has only now reminded me that your Mr Saunders telephoned just after you left yesterday. I told him you wouldn't be returning until late today and he asked that you ring him as soon as you got back.'

'Is that all? Heavens, you had me worried there for a moment. I thought it was something important and it's only dear Derek pining for me already and desperate for the sound of my voice.' Briony laughed at the vivid mental picture of Derek furious and fuming that she had not contacted him with a progress report on his precious collection. 'I'm surprised he hasn't turned up here in person.'

'The way he did last year, you mean?'

Morag's nervous look had come a second before Kyle's voice and Briony was already spinning around before he'd started speaking. While she saw, and heard, the hard-faced stranger in the doorway, her mind refused to connect him with the happy, loving Kyle she had left in the bedroom barely fifteen minutes ago. She just laughed. 'Darling, all——' She started to explain her flippant comments and stopped at the sharp close of the door which followed Morag's hasty departure from the kitchen to her own quarters. 'Kyle, all I meant was that——' she began again, and that was as far as she got.

'That he can't bear to be without you? Yes, so you've already made clear in that happy, unguarded little moment. And expecting him to turn up any moment now, are you—like last year when he came to persuade you back to London? He was pining for you then too, wasn't he? Although I didn't quite realise that at the time.' Kyle twisted a bitter smile at her frozen face. 'However, I did manage to catch on. Eventually.'

Briony unfroze enough to shake her head in amazement. 'You're talking nonsense, Kyle,' she protested, in exasperation almost, since what Kyle was implying was too preposterous to believe. 'Derek didn't need to persuade me back. You knew I hadn't planned to leave the business quite then. Not until we—the label—went into the US market.'

'The way it did into France, do you mean?' Kyle threw her completely with the mention of France— that he even remembered her talking about it, let alone that he was bringing it up now. 'That would have been the deal you stitched up in March, wouldn't it? If you'll pardon the pun.'

'No, not March, it was well before that,' she told him, bewildered, and sensing that something horrible was coming that she could see a mile off, but for the life of her Briony could not imagine what it could be.

'Oh, was it? I stand corrected.' What was so awful was Kyle sounding as if he was making light conversation at a party while all the time his eyes were so deadly that she was beginning to feel frightened. 'So the trip to Paris in March was just a private occasion for you and Saunders? Celebrating something special, were you, in that fancy hotel? Yes, I did happen to come to Paris myself.'

Kyle bared his teeth in a savage grin at her shock. 'You see, I'd convinced myself that I'd been unfair in jumping to my conclusions about why it was so important to you to remain in London. Even after finding you two so cosily together in our apartment, being strung the line about that trumped-up new collection, and your point-blank refusal to return to work from Barra, I was still prepared to believe I had been wrong about you and Saunders. Until Paris, that is.'

All the absurd, unfathomable innuendoes were no longer unfathomable, but more than ever absurd. She was having an affair with Derek? Was that what Kyle meant? It had to be. Briony just kept staring and shaking her head in disbelief at everything he was saying.

'Paris. . .?' she finally repeated weakly, because it seemed to hold some dreadful significance. 'You came to Paris. . .?'

'As soon as I got back from visiting Henrik in Norway and learnt that you'd been trying to contact me, yes. I rushed over the Channel to apologise for my unreasonableness and my suspicions of the previous six months. But the opportunity never came up. However——' Kyle shrugged dismissively '—it wasn't an entirely wasted trip because otherwise I could never have been certain, could I, about you and "dear Derek"? But there's nothing more certain-making than learning Ms Hayward and Mr Saunders are booked into the same room.'

'But it was a suite and——'

'Oh, quite,' Kyle interposed with venomous politeness, 'and with even enough room for me to have dossed down on the sofa, I dare say. I understand everybody is terribly sophisticated about these things in Paris—London too—and it's only in this little backwater that we're so boringly old-fashioned in our outlook. Which is no doubt why you couldn't—and still can't—wait to get away from here. Only you found you still rather fancied me, didn't you, as you showed me on Mingulay?' He moved towards her, and Briony shot around to the other side of Morag's large marble-topped table. Kyle's mouth twisted derisively at her over-reaction. 'You needn't alarm yourself, Briony. I'm not going to force myself on you. Our day on Mingulay was quite enough of a goodbye for me,' he added on a soft laugh while his eyes looked as if they hated her, and, although he was a good four feet or so away, she shrank back from him as if he had struck her. Her mind reeled at the words and any protest, any explanation she might have made about her supposed affair died unvoiced.

'You set it up.' She was not asking. Of course Kyle had set it up. And if she hadn't been so blinded by her hopes, and later her happiness, she might have taken in the trail of clues and recognised the trip for the set-up it had been. . . The mountain of stuff they had taken. . .no one being concerned. . . Morag telling Derek that she would only be back the next day. Everybody had known they'd set off to spend the night there, and so would she have if she hadn't been so blind to everything but Kyle. 'You set me up,' she repeated, her voice barely above an appalled whisper.

'Yes.'

'Stranded us there so I. . .we would. . .'

'That's right. So that we would.'

'Because you thought Derek and I. . .?' She couldn't finish. Kyle had made love to her to settle a score. To pay her back for her supposed affair with Derek. She must have looked as shattered as she felt, and as ill, because something went out of Kyle's face, and the taunting smile off it. 'I shall never forgive you for that, Kyle. Never.'

He moved to her suddenly. 'Briony, no, I ——'

CHAPTER TEN

BRIONY didn't wait to hear the rest. She rushed past him, out of the kitchen and out of the house, then had to take Kyle's car to get away because the key to hers was in her bag upstairs and she couldn't spare the time to dash up to get it. Kyle's key, as always, was in the ignition — a telling difference between her world in London and his on Barra, she had always thought. Now her only thought was to put as much distance between them as she could.

On the mainland, hours of driving would have seen her hundreds of miles away; on Barra, the few turn-offs from the ring road led only into the hills or to the water's edge, and there was no way off the island. With nowhere else left to go, she finally made her way into Castlebay, to be greeted by the sound of piping from the small hall at the side of the square. Another evening of entertainment in progress. . .of people enjoying themselves, and no one aware, or caring, that her whole world had just disintegrated. Even the castle, standing as solidly as ever in its sea, seemed to mock her with its enchantment, the charm of it gone for her, together with her dreams of a future with Kyle. Dreams as insubstantial as a castle in the air, based as they'd been on the love she had thought she had regained on Mingulay.

Love. . .? A cruel hoax. And how easy she had made it for him. She loved him and had wanted —

166

desperately—to make love with him; she could not deny that for a moment. And there had been no conditions attached. She had not asked for any guarantee of a reconciliation beforehand, and Kyle had not given any. Their lovemaking had come about spontaneously and had been wonderful. So she had believed—so Kyle had led her to believe while coldly, calculatingly, setting her up right from the start. Briony was afraid she would never be able to forgive him for that, when strangely perhaps, she would have readily forgiven the grotesque accusations if Kyle hàd confronted her in a blaze of anger or jealousy, because no matter how unfounded, how hurtful, at least they would have been based on love, or a love betrayed, in Kyle's view.

But any love he'd had for her had long disappeared, and if she needed more reinforcement of that painful truth she had it in the sight of his car parked outside the Macleods' pub. Not Kyle's car as much since she was driving it at that very moment; it was her own white Honda that he'd had to use to get himself to Ishabel this evening, not bothering any longer with even the pretence of keeping his distance from her while his wife was on the island.

There was a space between her car and the next. Briony abruptly swung the estate car into it and parked. Leaving the key in the ignition, she was opening the door to climb out, her intention to drive off in her own car—to where she had not got as far as thinking—when the door was suddenly swung open and held wide open for her. For one unnerving moment she thought it was by Kyle.

'Hello, Briony. Kyle not with you? Then come

along and have a drink with me.' Peter closed the door for her and took her arm. 'Is Kyle coming later? I want a word with him about something that has cropped up regarding the Feis.'

'He's here already.' Briony gestured distractedly towards the building while at the same time attempting to free herself of the firmly attached hand without seeming too obvious about it. 'I haven't come to. . . I mean, I only stopped to. . .' 'To change cars' would have embarrassed her more than she could have coped with. 'Look, Peter, I'd really rather not join you right now. I. . . I'm not dressed for it,' she tried again in sheer desperation as he shepherded her up the steep path to the building.

She had fled in sweater and jeans, soft leather slip-ons on her feet, and her hair loose and quite dry now after the hours of driving around. Altogether, she looked perfectly presentable for casual drinks in a pub and the excuse was so lame that it could have been taken as fishing for compliments.

'Not dressed for what? You're on Barra now and we don't much go in for formality here — as you should remember. And anyway, you look great — as always.' Peter accompanied the compliment with an appreciative once-over before steering her into the lounge. It was cheerfully noisy with voices and laughter, but, since it was vying with the evening's Feis function at the hall, only half-full. 'Kyle doesn't appear to be here.' Peter's quick survey of the room confirmed her own hasty scan. 'There's Ishabel, though; she'll know where he's got to.'

Yes. And how telling of the island's acceptance of that liaison that Peter should instantly have assumed

Ishabel would know. Briony was not up to an encounter with Ishabel, any more than with Kyle, and if there had been any capacity for surprise left in her she would have been surprised that the girl immediately began to hurry towards them, seemingly anxious for an encounter rather than doing her best to avoid one as Briony would have done in her place.

'Hi, Ishabel, have you seen Kyle about? Briony's come to join him and is wondering where he's vanished to. Do you know. . .?'

Briony was horrified to hear Peter putting words into her mouth that she would have choked on. She met Ishabel's steady gaze and gave a mute shake of denial.

'He's in our private sitting-room making a phone call to Reef House. I'll take you to him,' said Ishabel quietly, but very firmly.

Oh, God, she thinks I've turned up to make a scene and doesn't want it in the public lounge, thought Briony suddenly and felt the sweep of humiliation setting her cheeks on fire as fiercely as if she had actually tracked Kyle down to his girlfriend, hell-bent on a confrontation, instead of having been all but carried in by thoughtless, genial Peter.

'No.' She shook her head wildly. 'No. Oh, no.' The gurgling little laughs punctuating the string of 'no's frightened her into thinking she was beginning to lose her grip on herself, and just when she needed her dignity the most. Briony pulled herself together by sheer will-power. 'No, thank you, Ishabel, that isn't necessary. And I'm afraid I can't stay any longer. I was on my way to. . .somewhere else, and not looking for Kyle at all.' She spoke directly to

Ishabel and was backing away at the same time, desperate to make her escape, before Kyle returned.

'Were you not? Dear me, then it looks as if I've kidnapped you.' Peter finally caught on, thought it funny and laughed. 'But now that we're all here, can we discuss Sunday's games for a minute or two — the prize-giving part, I mean?'

'I'm sorry, but I'll have left Barra by then. I'm flying back to London tomorrow and really must get home to pack. Perhaps Ishabel can help you out with the prize-giving?' She smiled a quite madly bright smile at them before rushing from the room, and, having rushed out, realised again that there was nowhere for her to go.

Tomorrow, just as she had told the baffled pair, she would fly out. If there wasn't a spare seat on the scheduled flight, she would charter a plane from the mainland; her car could follow by ferry — or stay on Barra forever, Briony didn't care, so long as she herself got off the island. But that could only be tomorrow and in the meantime she would have to return to Reef House, if only to pack. For the moment, though, Briony could not face it. Nor any more of the aimless driving, nor sitting in the car in one of the little villages tucked away on the western side of the island, or on its northern tip, staring across at the tiny island of Eriskay and feeling helpless because she couldn't reach it to get away from Kyle. She turned into the Street and drove the Honda right down to the pier, which was deserted, and, temporarily, at least, as isolated as the most isolated of crannies anywhere on the island.

There was a bench against the side-wall of the last

building of the row of shops that fronted the Street. Facing only the castle and the bay, it was out of sight of anyone further up the Street, and, while the gathering dusk indicated that it must be around ten o'clock, it was still rather early for young lovers to come in search of privacy, and romance. And they would not have heralded their arrival with a slam of a car door that sent shock-waves through the stillness of the evening and almost made her jump out of her skin.

It could only be Kyle. She tensed, waiting, and had already turned away from the sound of his frantic footsteps before he came pounding around the corner of the building.

'Where have you been? I've been all over the island looking for you, leaving messages every-where — not to mention telephoning Morag every ten minutes to ask if you were back.'

Briony turned her eyes to him in a dull stare.

'Don't you realise I've been worried out of my mind not knowing where you'd gone, and terrified something might have happened to you?'

Kyle worried, and angry with her for causing him the worry. . .? It made her want to laugh, and she did a little, and then, the next moment, was laughing and weeping together as the last of her precarious self-control disintegrated. 'But that's just it. I can't go anywhere. I can't get off the island.'

'Thank God for that.' Kyle was beside her on the bench, gathering her into his arms and just holding her and hushing her, and all Briony was aware of was that she felt comforted and safe in his arms and she didn't want to feel that way — must not let herself feel that way. She had to leave Barra firmly focused on the cruel, insensitive Kyle who had set her up so calculatingly. . .the Kyle she didn't know any more and who would never be allowed to hurt her again. She wrenched her face away from his chest and the familiar navy wool of his sweater, and pulled herself out of the embrace, but had to remain under the one arm tightly around her shoulder when Kyle refused to remove it.

'I'm fine now. Thank you,' she mumbled and tried to stand up to sever the disturbing physical contact. 'I'll be leaving on the plane tomorrow, so——'

Kyle's arm drew her back down instantly, and closer in to his side. 'I don't want you to leave, Briony. Not tomorrow, not ever. I love you,' he added simply, and stopped her heart in its tracks.

She swung her face to him. 'No,' she shot back quickly before the tiniest hope could get the chance to push its way through the disbelief. She shook her head angrily. 'No, Kyle, you don't love me. How can you say that? After all the things you've believed about me? After Mingulay. . .?' A tremulousness had crept into her voice and Briony knew she was pleading. . .for explanations, rationalisations—anything so that she could give in and believe him, believe that in spite of everything it was possible that Kyle loved her. How could she still be so vulnerable to him. . .? Because she loved him, and there was nothing she could do about it.

Agitatedly twisting herself out from under his arm, she sprang up from the bench and began walking rapidly towards the pier. 'You set me up,' she accused him when he caught up with her and pulled her to a stop.'You admitted it. You set me up just for sex. Because you believed I was going back to Derek and——' She was crying at him more in despair now than in accusation.

Kyle's face contorted with the groan. 'Oh, God, no. I mean, yes, I did fake the "stranding"—set you up, if that's how you want to put it—but not for sex. Because I love you and wanted to make it easier for you to tell me that you loved me too. . .so that we could resolve things between us. And I thought we had—until I overheard you talking to Morag and jumped to my conclusions. Wrong conclusions, yes,' Kyle admitted quickly before she could interject. 'I realised that from your reactions, your face, and should have realised it when I overheard you in the first place—that you'd hardly be telling Morag "dear Derek" was pining for you—and meaning it.'

'There has never been any affair between Derek and me. Not at any time. Not even before I met you,' Briony added vehemently, as an extra assurance, and so intent on convincing Kyle that there had never been any basis for his doubts about her that she was unaware that she was stating the obvious.

A little of the tautness went from Kyle's face as the faint trace of a smile flickered across his lips. 'Darling, I did realise that no other man had ever made love to you,' he told her gently. 'And believe me, the thought that there might be any possibility of it happening after we were married never crossed my mind. Which was why it was such a shock when everything seemed to stack up so damnably neatly once the first doubt had lodged in.'

Kyle stood looking at her, his face shadowed, as well as partially in shadow as he stood with the brooding of the castle behind his own dark figure, and for the first time Briony realised that she was the only one to have been caused pain by Kyle's doubts and suspicions.

'I thought you didn't want me. Didn't love me any more,' she confessed simply.

Her face was caught between his hands and her mouth under Kyle's for the unexpected kiss that was hard and sweet and went on forever as Kyle sought to reassure her while Ishabel clung to him as if she could never be reassured enough.

'I never stopped loving you, or wanting you,' he actually told her at last when they finally broke apart, and only then did she notice that they were fully on the pier and easily seen from the road if anyone happened to be passing by. 'And when you returned to Barra last week, all the signs pointed to you still loving me too — or at least wanting me,' Kyle qualified as he slipped an arm around her shoulder to lead them back to the street end of the pier and then to the cars. 'Your body told me that every time I touched you, and you would have let me seduce you, *mo gràdh*, we both know that. Only I needed more from you. After all my doubts, I needed you to make the move, to tell me of your own accord — and in your own time — that you loved me and wanted to return to me for good. And to help you along —— ' Kyle's voice lightened perceptibly ' — I was going to keep you here — one devious way or another — until you did tell me.'

'By setting up Mingulay with a faked stranding.'
Briony could smile now.

About to open the passenger door of his estate
car, Kyle flashed a sudden grin. 'Yes, that too. And
it's a pity we — or rather I — didn't make full use of it
to resolve everything once and for all. But as far as I
was concerned, the past didn't matter any longer and
there was no point in resurrecting it, so I let the
opportunity pass when you led around to affairs.'

Affairs — plural, not singular. They had resolved
her 'affair', and only that.

'We'll have your car collected tomorrow,' Kyle
said as he handed her into his car.

She gave him a quick look and climbed in, conscious of her own new tension, and not sure she
would be able to keep Kyle from noticing it, or
suspecting its cause. It should not have mattered,
surely. Kyle loved her. She was in no doubt about
that any more. And if he had turned to Ishabel
during their estrangement. . .? It was irrational to
want to know for certain, yet if she didn't Briony was
afraid that there would always be a lingering shadow
in some dark recess of her mind, ready to spring
forward whenever she saw them together, and set
her wondering how much they had meant to each
other.

They had just started up the Street when Kyle
pulled the car to an abrupt stop outside the post
office.

He made no move to get out of the car. 'We
haven't finished yet, have we? Look at me, Briony,'
he ordered when she kept staring ahead, watching
the flurry of activity in the square as people prepared

to leave for home after the evening's function in the hall.

She turned to him in a sort of defeat, realising that Kyle had sensed her tension and somehow deduced what was behind it.

'I did not have an affair with Ishabel Macleod.'

'I didn't think you——' she began to protest out of habit. 'I mean I only. . .wondered.' She changed the protest into a semi-confession.

Kyle smiled grimly. 'After my own suspicions, I'm in no position to blame anybody else for theirs, but darling, wherever your suspicions have come from, there's never been any basis for them,' he assured her adamantly. 'Yes, I have seen a lot of Ishabel, but only because I've spent so much time playing chess with Dugald—her father—since he moved his family to Barra. And he did that to get Ishabel away from Harris, and all its associations for her after her fiancé drowned in a fishing-boat accident last year.'

'Oh, no.' Briony interjected, shocked. 'Oh, the poor girl. I had no idea.'

'How could you unless you talked to her? And she's not given to opening up about it. She did to me eventually, possibly because she felt comfortable with me after she realised I was about the only male on the island who had no intention of bombarding her with unwelcome advances.'

Briony believed him, and gladly, and yet Kyle's explanation didn't explain everything. She had not imagined those frigid stares, the beautiful black eyes coldly looking through her. 'But she seemed to. . . resent me.'

'Resent you?' Kyle repeated, astonished. 'Good

grief. Where did you pick up that odd idea? At the airport? The tatties and herring night. . .? They're the only times you've seen each other, aren't they? Oh, and the ceilidh.'

Where Kyle had obviously missed Ishabel's see-through glance at her. 'There was another time — the evening I dined at the pub. With Martin. I — we — saw her there.'

'Ah,' said Kyle as if something had become clear to him. 'With Martin Gunn — the one man on the island Ishabel is interested in now that she's about ready to form a new relationship! And you turn up and seem about to haul him off. The poor girl must have wondered what was going on.'

Everything fell into place at last, including Kyle's curious insistence that she keep away from Martin. Briony stopped short of telling him what Martin had got into his head about Ishabel and Kyle himself. It wasn't important any more. 'I designed the Hebridean Collection around Ishabel.' She confessed on a sudden impulse what she considered her masochistic little secret, and was chagrined when Kyle smiled.

'Yes, I know. I saw your sketchpad when you left it in the pocket of my jacket, and thought the muse had struck in a rather unexpected way. Why don't you show her the sketches? They were great and I think she'd get a real kick out of them.'

'Yes, I might do that,' Briony murmured. And later she might suggest to Derek that he consider using Ishabel as a model, if Ishabel herself was agreeable to it.

Kyle leaned over and gave her a light kiss. 'Enough. I'm taking you home now.' He started up the car again, got as far as the square and had to screech to a stop to avoid hitting the man who appeared to launch himself straight at the vehicle. 'What the devil is Peter doing throwing himself under my wheels?' Kyle wound down the window. 'Trying to commit suicide, are you?' he growled when Peter poked his red head through the opening.

'Sorry about that but I didn't want to miss you. I noticed you both enjoying your walk along the pier earlier and I didn't want to disturb you then,' he grinned, and Briony blushed madly, knowing his description of their activity was a euphemism for the passionate kiss he — and goodness knew how many others — had witnessed. 'It's about Sunday. In view of Briony leaving Barra tomorrow, I wanted——'

'Briony is not leaving tomorrow. Whatever gave you that idea?'

Peter drew his head back slightly, and, avoiding a direct stare into her embarrassed face, muttered to Kyle, 'Och, I thought someone mentioned something about it. Obviously they had their facts wrong.'

'Entirely,' confirmed Kyle shortly.

'In that case, you'll be available to give out the prizes, Briony. . .?' He looked across at her now and grinned cheerfully.

'Yes. Thank you for asking me.' Again, she meant, and for being so tactful about her earlier odd behaviour in the pub.

'Did you put him up to it? Suggest to Peter that he ask me. . .?' she asked, curious, as they left Peter and the town behind them.

Kyle's surprise was genuine. 'No. What makes you ask that?'

'I thought. . .well, when you insisted I go to the tatties and herring night with you that you might have fixed it with Peter that he ask me. That it might have been one of your devious ways of keeping me on the island at least until Sunday.'

Kyle shook his head. 'No, I didn't fix it. Peter asked you because he wanted to. Because you're very much part of this place — which is what I wanted to prove to you when I suggested that we go that night. . .show you how very much you fitted in, and belonged here with me.'

'Oh.' Briony thought that over for a moment. 'Then your only deviousness about keeping me here was in arranging the "stranding". . .?'

'Not quite,' Kyle admitted with a grin. 'There was the small matter of the ferry.'

'The sheep!' Briony burst out laughing. 'There wasn't going to be any pick-up of sheep and I could have left on Tuesday.'

'Oh, the sheep sailed right enough. It was Saturday you could have left. The ferry was due to sail half-empty — as I was horribly afraid you'd find out if you'd thought to doubt my word and telephone the pier office. But then,' Kyle went on with a smile in his voice, 'I would simply have resorted to a bit of night driving and drilled a hole into the side of the ferry. There was no way you were going to be leaving this island, my darling.'

'Kyle. . .?'

'Hmm?'

Propped up on her elbow beside him, Briony

trailed a finger lightly down his bare spine and back up again.

Kyle rolled over and started to reach for her.

She drew back from him. 'No, darling, I want to talk.'

It was well into morning. They had made love earlier. She had been wakened by the familiar, thrilling sensation of Kyle's mouth tugging sensuously at her breast, and, from then on, most of the morning had vanished in a haze of lovemaking that had covered the gamut of all the love they had ever made—from the most tender to the most wildly passionate.

There had been something different about their lovemaking today, though. They had made love on Mingulay yesterday, but not last night when they returned to Reef House. Both emotionally and physically exhausted by the day's events, they had simply gone to bed and fallen asleep securely in each other's arms, both knowing that they had all the time in the world for love. . .lovemaking. And this morning it had been like a celebration—a confirmation of that, unlike yesterday on Mingulay, where it had been a love declared but in a way not confirmed, with their separate doubts and secret thoughts between them still. Briony had only realised that difference this morning.

She sat up against the pillows so that Kyle wouldn't draw her down to himself and make her put off what she needed to discuss.

'I'm listening, *m'eudail*.' He looked up at her expectantly.'

'I have to go back to London, Kyle,' Briony

plunged straight in. 'Only for a few weeks,' she added quickly, watching his face nervously for reaction. . .for the tightening of muscles, clouding of eyes.

'I know.'

'Just to finalise the business and see the Hebridean—— Oh.' She registered what Kyle had just said. 'Then you don't mind?'

He sat up beside her. 'No, since I'm coming with you and staying with you until you finish whatever it is you have to see through. Is that all you wanted to talk about?' He smiled at her surprise, his hand sliding up and down her bare thigh underneath the quilt.

'Well, yes. Well, no,' she amended, not entirely reassured by his ready acceptance of her need to return. 'Kyle, I do want to carry on with my career— work freelance from Barra, I mean.'

Kyle frowned at her as if he had trouble understanding her. It was the same expression he'd worn when she had railed at him about her career on the morning of the ceilidh when they'd had that dreadful row and she had accused him of being anti her career.

'Of course you'll be continuing with your career,' he told her as if she had been expressing doubts about such a course. 'How could you not? It's a part of you. Part of the vital, passionate and very talented woman I fell instantly in love with. Of course I want you to continue using your talent. That's what talent is for—to be used. And expanded into new directions when the time is right.'

It was Briony's turn to frown. 'New directions. . .? What new directions, Kyle?'

'Oh, I was thinking of new ranges. Like maternity wear. It is possible you might consider a range such as that in the near future, isn't it?'

She was already eased down from the pillows, Kyle's body over her. Briony smiled into his eyes. 'Very possible,' she assured him. 'And it will be my best collection yet.'

Welcome to Europe

BARRA — 'the most beautiful little island in Britain'

It's official! Barra was given this title in the 1980s after a nationwide poll — and you're sure to agree. It's a stunning landscape of wide white beaches and dramatic mountains, picturesque castles and isolated settlements. Of course it's the perfect place for a peaceful, get-away-from-it-all holiday, but there's also plenty to see and do, and it's one of the best places to soak yourself in romantic and fascinating Celtic culture and history.

THE ROMANTIC PAST

Barra is part of the **Outer Hebrides** — the western outpost of Great Britain. The islands have a turbulent history, having suffered many years of **Viking** domination in the Dark Ages: the Norsemen established a garrison on Barra as it was a convenient base for their pillaging raids on Ireland. Echoes of their presence on the island remain in many of the place names.

St Columba, who is famous for the conversion of Britain to Christianity, may never have visited Barra, but the island boasts a holy spring named in his honour, which, it has been claimed, will ensure good catches for fishermen, and also cure the sick. The island was actually named for his follower **St Barr**, who also has a well to his name—this one produced when he struck the ground with his staff.

Barra is perhaps more famous throughout the English-speaking world as the headquarters of the **Clan Macneil**. Scots have always been renowned for their energy and enterprise, and the people of Barra are certainly no exception; the island has produced sailors who have journeyed to the most distant parts of the globe. Many people also left involuntarily in the tragic 'Highland Clearances' of the eighteenth and nineteenth centuries, forced away by poverty to make a new life, particularly in Canada and the US. Yet the descendants of many of these emigrants retain strong ties with their ancestral home. The 45th Chief of the Clan Macneil was an American, Robert Lister Macneil, and his son has inherited the title. The Macneils were able to reacquire and restore their ancient home, **Kisimul Castle**—one of the oldest inhabited castles in Scotland, and probably the most beautiful—and now host a grand **gathering of the Clan** every ten years. Macneils take note: the next one is scheduled for **1997**. . .and you're all welcome!

In ancient times the Macneils were famous for their self-confidence (to put it mildly!). It is said that after the chief had eaten, his herald would proclaim:

> Hear o ye people and listen all ye nations
> The great Macneil of Barra having finished his
>   meal
> The princes of the world may now dine!

Barra — being so photogenic — has featured in many films and TV programmes, but its most famous appearance remains the classic black and white film **WHISKY GALORE**. This was based on a book by local author **Sir Compton Mackenzie** which he took from a true story; during the Second World War a ship carrying a large cargo of whisky was wrecked off the island and the cargo mysteriously disappeared, owing to the enormous ingenuity of the inhabitants! The **Cliat Caves**, in which some of the missing whisky was allegedly hidden, can still be seen — at low tide!

THE ROMANTIC PRESENT — pastimes for lovers. . .

If you arrive on Barra by **plane**, your holiday will get off to a fascinating start before you even set foot on the island: the flight schedule is determined by the pattern of the tides here, because the planes actually land on the beautiful shell **beach**!

The main town and social centre of the island is charming little **Castlebay**. From here you can take a short boat trip to visit the lovely sea-girt Kisimul Castle — one of the most photographed sights in the whole of Scotland. Opinions differ as to when it was built; the Macneils believe it dates as far back as **AD 1030**. If the Chief of the Clan is in residence, his flag will be flying.

Barra is a paradise for **walkers**, whether it's a gentle stroll or something more strenuous you have in mind. There are many atmospheric ancient **forts** and mysterious **standing stones** which are well worth a visit. And Barra is famous for its **wildlife**: for bird-watchers, it plays host to around 150 species of bird, some of which are rarely seen elsewhere, and it is also made beautiful by over a thousand types of wild flower.

Despite being so far north, the sea around the island is not as cold as you might expect, because of the proximity of the **Gulf Stream**. The beaches are simply stunning in their unspoilt beauty, and if you *are* brave enough for a swim you may find yourself in the company of a friendly and curious **seal**!

For many people, the main attraction of Barra is its lively and vibrant Celtic culture. If you're lucky enough to visit in **early July** you'll find the island bustling with activity as it's the time of the annual local festival or **Feis**. The programme features theme dinners of traditional local foods, plays, exhibitions, and of course the famous highland **ceilidhs** — evenings of singing, folk dancing and music. Traditional instruments include the **fiddle**, **bagpipes**, and the *clarsach*—the small Gaelic harp which is so popular with children. Barra is known as a specially musical island, so you should be in for a treat—and maybe you'll be invited to participate as well as watch!

However you spend your days on Barra, you're sure to work up a healthy appetite in the clean and bracing air. And you're in the right place when it comes to food! The whole of Scotland is rightly famous for the freshness and quality of its produce, but Barra is particularly well known for its wonderful **salmon** and **lobster**—salmon is farmed in the bays around the island, and couldn't be fresher! The local drink is of course **whisky**—in Gaelic, *uisge beatha*—'the water of life'.

One of the great pleasures of Barra is browsing round the unique little shops. Gifts to be found include beautiful **jewellery** in the ancient Celtic designs, with their lovely flowing lines: what better present for a loved one than a ring showing the famous 'knot of eternity'—a symbol of undying love? You should also watch out for cosy **handknitted sweaters** (you may need them if the weather proves unpredictable!) and the celebrated **tweed** from nearby **Harris**. But the best souvenirs of Barra will surely be your memories. . .

DID YOU KNOW THAT. . .?

* Barra is nearer the **North Pole** than **Moscow**.

* as it's so far north, in the summer it doesn't get dark — the nights consist of five hours of twilight at the most.

* Barra has **no traffic-lights**!

* **Gaelic** is now taught in schools alongside English, and is therefore growing in popularity.

* the **Scottish currency** is the same as the English, except that Scottish banks print their own notes — which are much prettier than English ones! — and have retained the **pound note**, which has been phased out in England.

* 'I love you' in Gaelic is '*Tha gàol agam ort*'.

LOOK OUT FOR TWO TITLES EVERY MONTH IN OUR SERIES OF EUROPEAN ROMANCES:

DANGEROUS DESIRE: Sarah Holland (Monaco)
Isabelle adored Monaco — but hated Jean-Luc. But he *was* incredibly handsome, and seemed to want to help. Could she trust him?

BITTER MEMORIES: Margaret Mayo (Tenerife)
Tanya was shocked to bump into Alejandro Vazquez Herrera the moment she arrived in Tenerife — she hadn't expected ever to see him again. Could she resist him second time around?

THE SULTAN'S FAVOURITE: Helen Brooks (Turkey)
Louisa had run to Turkey to escape the past, and run straight into Melik Haman! He swept her off her feet — but could Louisa hope to find a permanent place in his heart?

LEAP OF FAITH: Rachel Elliot (Jersey)
The notorious Marc Duval had decided that Tessa was just what he needed — but did she really need *him*? He was using her, and she knew it, but found it hard to resist him. . .

Accept 4 FREE Romances and 2 FREE gifts

FROM READER SERVICE

Here's an irresistible invitation from
Mills & Boon. Please accept our offer of
4 FREE Romances, a CUDDLY TEDDY
and a special MYSTERY GIFT!
Then, if you choose, go on to enjoy 6
captivating Romances every month for
just £1.90 each, postage and packing
FREE. Plus our FREE Newsletter
with author news, competitions
and much more.

Send the coupon below to:
Mills & Boon Reader Service,
FREEPOST, PO Box 236,
Croydon, Surrey CR9 9EL.

NO STAMP REQUIRED

Yes! Please rush me 4 FREE Romances and 2 FREE gifts! Please also
reserve me a Reader Service subscription. If I decide to subscribe I can look
forward to receiving 6 brand new Romances for just £11.40 each month, post and
packing FREE. If I decide not to subscribe I shall write to you within 10 days -
I can keep the free books and gifts whatever I choose. I may cancel or suspend my
subscription at any time. I am over 18 years of age.

Ms/Mrs/Miss/Mr _____ EP70R

Address _____

_____

Postcode _____ Signature _____

mps
MAILING
PREFERENCE
SERVICE